THE

Kien was carrying the ice cream for Mai's
first American birthday when he saw the
redhead waiting, a gleam in his hating eyes.
Two more boys came up behind him. One
carried a metal pipe.

Suddenly Kien was back in Saigon, reacting
with street-wise instinct. A scrabble in the
dust, a heavy stone in his hand, a swift leap.
The redhead screamed in pain . . .

Kien was safe. But he knew his wonderful life
in his adopted home would never be the
same. Even here there was hate . . .

A Long Way from Home

MAUREEN CRANE WARTSKI

Ⓢ
A SIGNET BOOK

SIGNET
Published by the Penguin Group
Penguin Books USA Inc , 375 Hudson Street.
New York, New York 10014, U.S.A
Penguin Books Ltd. 27 Wrights Lane.
London W8 5TZ. England
Penguin Books Australia Ltd. Ringwood.
Victoria, Australia
Penguin Books Canada Ltd. 10 Alcorn Avenue.
Toronto, Ontario, Canada M4V 3B2
Penguin Books (N.Z.) Ltd. 182–190 Wairau Road.
Auckland 10, New Zealand

Penguin Books Ltd. Registered Offices.
Harmondsworth, Middlesex, England

This is an authorized reprint of a hardcover edition
published by The Westminster Press.

First Signet Printing, February, 1982
14 13 12 11 10 9 8 7 6

 REGISTERED TRADEMARK—MARCA REGISTRADA

Printed in the United States of America

PUBLISHER'S NOTE
This is a work of fiction. Names, characters, places, and incidents either are the product
of the author's imagination or are used fictitiously, and any resemblance to actual
persons, living or dead, events, or locales is entirely coincidental.

BOOKS ARE AVAILABLE AT QUANTITY DISCOUNTS WHEN USED TO PROMOTE PRODUCTS OR SERVICES
FOR INFORMATION PLEASE WRITE TO PREMIUM MARKETING DIVISION. PENGUIN BOOKS USA INC 375
HUDSON STREET NEW YORK. NEW YORK 10014.

For Ju, Joe, and Miyochan

1

As Kien left the refugee camp and made his way into the city, the sun was just beginning to touch the sloping roofs and to sparkle on the waters that separated Kowloon from Hong Kong Island beyond. The road was crowded with refugee men and women and older children like Kien, who were going to jobs in the city. If only he could find a job too! He needed the money badly.

He stopped one of the women and asked for directions and advice. "Aunt," he said, "I need to find a medicine seller named Ah Lin in the city. Our friend in the camp, Lam, says that Ah Lin's medicine has helped her grandson's cough. I need the medicine for my sister."

"Be careful of that one," the woman cautioned Kien. "These storekeepers are all the same. They double the price when they see you are a poor refugee."

"Ah Lin is dishonest," a man added, "but so is Son Kee, another seller of medicines. It is said that they are bitter rivals and always trying to steal customers from each other. They are greedy men!"

Kien next asked where a job might be found. Some refugees who worked at the Diamond Company's factory suggested he try there. "They hire many people, including youngsters. The pay is not much, but when one is poor, one cannot pick and choose."

The pay was terrible, but Kien knew that with a few Hong Kong dollars he could buy medicine for Mai. Maybe, with medicine, her terrible cough would get better. He settled down to his day's work with a sigh.

The work—stringing hairpins onto small cardboard rectangles—was tedious. Kien was soon bored and tired. His arms and legs ached, the factory was badly lighted, and the air was so stale and stuffy that he could hardly breathe. Many times Kien was tempted to throw away his pins and papers and to run away, but the memory of Mai's cough and her thin, frail body kept him where he was.

At the end of the workday, Kien took his day's wages and hurried out into the city. The sun was almost setting, but the factory had been so dark that daylight hurt Kien's eyes. He began to stroll along, taking in the crowded shops with their brightly painted signs, the bustle of people and traffic. Delicious smells of fried pork and chicken came from a food vendor on a street corner, and Kien's stomach growled hungrily. He thought of the dollars in his pocket, then shook his head. I will see this Ah Lin first, he thought.

Ah Lin's store was not far from the Diamond Company factory. It was a large store, and its shop window was crammed with all sorts of good things: medicines, cosmetics, candies, even toys. In the back of the window display hung a huge dragon kite. Kien thought of his little brother.

I'd like to get that for Loc, Kien said to himself. I wonder how much it costs.

He walked into the store and went up to the counter where a short, fat man with a scanty beard stood arranging bottles of medicine. Suddenly, it struck Kien that it wasn't going to be easy trading with Ah Lin. He didn't speak Chinese, and Ah Lin couldn't understand Vietnamese! But the little, fat man glanced once at Kien and cleared his throat.

"What will it be?" he asked in reasonably good Vietnamese. "Candy? A toy?"

"I need medicine for my sister's cough," Kien said. Ah Lin wagged his head gravely. "I was told to come here by a woman from the camp. A woman called Lam."

"Ah, ah," Ah Lin said, shaking his head still more. "My medicine for coughs is good. It is famous. It is expensive!"

Kien remembered what he had been told about Ah Lin's greed. Inwardly he chuckled, but he pulled his face into a sad mask and whispered, "But, good Uncle, I have no money. I am a poor Vietnamese refugee, an orphan. I have nothing but these bare hands."

Ah Lin named a price. Kien pretended to be horrified. "It cannot be! For such as me, this medicine is too expensive!" he cried. Then, raising his voice he added, "I must go to the shop of Son Kee after all."

Ah Lin frowned. It didn't matter to him where Kien went, but just then several customers had walked into his store. Kien continued, in an even louder voice, "Son Kee has a heart. He doesn't charge people too much! Son Kee is an honest man!"

Ah Lin saw his customers looking at one another. They did not understand Vietnamese, but they understood the name "Son Kee" and they could see Kien was upset. Kien shook his fist at Ah Lin.

"Son Kee would not take advantage of a poor orphan!" he shouted. "I will tell everyone to go to Son Kee's shop!"

Ah Lin was ready to strangle Kien. "Very well . . . Take the medicine for half the price, only get out of the shop!" he hissed.

Kien grinned, and dropped some money onto the shop counter before Ah Lin. "Now, Uncle," he said, "how much is that dragon kite in the window?"

A few moments later Kien left Ah Lin's shop with the bottle of medicine in his hand and the kite under his arm. He was in a wonderful mood. "That fat storekeeper

wanted to cheat me," he chuckled out loud, "me, Kien!"
He couldn't wait to see Loc's face when he saw the kite.

On the way back to the camp, Kien did some sightsee-
ing. He coaxed a bit of pork from the streetcorner food
vendor and a few flowers from an old woman who sold
flowers nearby. He stuck the flowers into his pocket for
Mai, and munched on the good, crisp pork as he
marched along the road. When he came within sight of
the camp, he saw that Mai and Loc were waiting for
him.

"Kien, Kien!" Loc shouted, pelting down the road
toward him. "Wonderful news! Lam and Hoa and Hang
are going to America! They got the news today. And we
got a letter—a letter from Steve Olson! He says we will
be going to America, too!"

Mai was also hurrying up. Her eyes were very bright.
"What's happening?" Kien asked her. "What's this about
a letter from Steve Olson?"

"The news came today, Kien. Steve spoke with his
wife and son and they want to sponsor us. It will take
some time, but we will be going to America . . . like
Lam and her grandchildren."

Kien felt a little dizzy with all this good news. "Where
is the letter?" he asked. But before Mai could answer,
Loc noticed the dragon kite. He gave such a loud yell
that several people poked their heads out of the camp
windows and doors to see what was going on.

"Is that for me?" Loc screamed. "For me?"

"Yes." Kien had no time to say anything else. Loc
snatched the kite from under Kien's arm and made off
with it. Up went the kite into the air, dwarfing little
Loc, who raced along on his short, skinny legs. Mai
burst out laughing, and Kien laughed, too. They laughed
so hard that they clung to each other for support,
laughed till the tears came and Mai began to cough.
Then Mai rested her cheek on Kien's shoulder and began to cry.

"We will really go to America, then," she whispered.
"It isn't a dream!"

Kien took Mai to their living area and gave her some of the medicine and made her rest. While he was doing this, old Lam came up, puffing and panting. She gave Kien and Mai a huge hug.

"I am having a party tonight," she announced. "You'll come? Everyone I know is coming. After nearly a year in this camp, we are finally going to America. I feel so happy I am sure I will burst!"

Kien nodded jubilantly. What a good day this was! The medicine for Mai . . . the letter . . . Lam's good news. "Of course we will come!" he declared.

The party was a happy one. Lam knew many people in the camp, and they all came to wish her and her grandchildren well. As Lam passed out tea and sweets to her guests, they gave her little gifts—an orange, a tiny hair comb for Hang, a wooden truck for Hoa. "Don't forget us when you get to America," they all said, and Kien knew all of them were hoping that their turn to leave the crowded camp would come soon.

One man had a harmonica. After the tea-drinking and the gift-giving, he played some songs and they sang together. He played popular songs at first, songs he had learned from the television. Then, later, he played songs from home, from Vietnam. Kien saw Mai's eyes fill with tears as they all sang the familiar tunes, and he slid his hand into his shirt to cradle the bag of precious Vietnamese sand that hung around his neck. No, Grandfather, he said to himself, none of us will forget our country.

The party lasted for several hours, but eventually they all drifted back to their own living areas. Kien was tired from the long, exciting day, yet he could not fall asleep. He kept thinking about Steve Olson's letter and remembering the kind, gentle blond American who had rescued them from the sea. That had been nearly six months ago, and to Kien those six months had seemed like six years! He was also kept awake by Mai's and Hoa's coughing. The medicine he had bought from Ah Lin did not seem to be doing Mai very much good.

The next morning, Kien went back to work for the Diamond Company. When he returned, Lam was telling Loc and Mai about her day. She and her grandchildren had had their medical examination, and there had been needles and questions and a strange machine before which they had been required to stand.

"The doctor said that this machine could look into our bodies and see our bones." Lam sniffed. "I didn't trust it."

Kien grinned. "But you must have faced the machine before, Aunt," he said. "Doctors saw us when we first came to this camp, remember? They stuck needles in us and took our blood and asked questions."

Lam sniffed. "I may be an ignorant old woman, but I cannot see what good it does to look at anyone's bones! My bones are my own business," she snapped. "These doctors are too nosy. They asked a lot of questions about Hoa's cough."

Kien looked at Hoa, who lay half asleep in Lam's lap. The little boy's face was flushed and he did not look very strong. "What did they say about his cough?" Kien asked.

"They said nothing of any use . . . just asked questions!" Lam complained. Then she added, "Well, that part is over, now. All we need to do is wait for the plane to America!"

The next few days were days of waiting for Kien, Loc, and Mai as well. Kien continued to work in the daytime, but in the evenings they would pull out Steve Olson's letter and read it over and over. Then they would look at the photograph of Steve, standing beside a blond-haired woman and a small fair-haired boy about Loc's age.

"We will be waiting to welcome you when the time comes for you to come to America," Steve had written. "I have spoken with one of the agencies that help settle Vietnamese refugees in America. Since I was on the ship that rescued you from the sea, and since we can offer what you need, they have agreed to let Diane and Tad and me be your sponsors in this country. We have your rooms ready, and although our house is small, I know we will all enjoy living together."

Kien and Mai read this part over many times. "How can a house be small and yet have so many rooms?" Mai asked Kien. "Doesn't it say here that 'our rooms' are ready?"

"Maybe Steve doesn't write Vietnamese too well," Kien suggested. Mai nodded.

"Perhaps that's it. Oh, Kien, doesn't the lady have a kind face? Diane . . . it is a nice name." She tried the strange name out a few times. "I can't wait to—"

Her words were interrupted by a loud wail. Kien started in dismay as he saw Lam running toward them. The big woman's face was contorted, and she carried Hoa in her arms. Behind her, little Hang wept bitterly.

"Aunt!" Mai and Kien shouted together, and Loc, who had been playing with his kite nearby, came running up to ask, "What is wrong?"

Lam sank down on Mai's cot and buried her face in her big hands. "They will not let us go to America," she moaned.

Mai and Kien stared at her in horror. "Why?" Loc cried.

"It is Hoa. My poor little grandson is sick. That horrible machine that sees into a person's bones found a spot on his lung." Lam now began to rock to and fro in her grief. "He can't go to America till he is cured of this spot on his lung. They will take us from this camp and put Hoa in a hospital. It is a bitter life under this Heaven. A bitter, bitter life . . ."

Mai could not say a word. She put her arms around Lam and tried to comfort the big woman. Kien tried to speak bravely. "It won't be long before Hoa gets well. You'll be in America soon," he said.

Hoa began to cry, too, and it was more than Kien could stand. He turned away. But Loc darted forward and pushed his dragon kite into Hoa's small hands.

"Take care of it for me till we see you again," he said breathlessly. Then he, too, burst into tears.

That night, in the darkness, Kien listened to Mai's raspy breathing. He waited for her cough to start, and he tensed as her breathing changed, grew harsh. "Mai?" he asked, afraid.

Mai didn't answer, but Kien could hear her sob. He reached out and took her hand. It was cold and felt so thin and weak in his. "Mai, are you crying about Lam?"

"Yes . . . no . . . I'm crying for me, too. Kien, I cough like Hoa. Supposing, when it's time for us to be examined, that machine sees a spot on my lung?"

Kien felt something cold and hard form in the apple of his throat. He said fiercely, "That's nonsense. Your cough is not as bad as Hoa's. That medicine is helping you."

"Kien," Mai said, "if I am sick, I want you and Loc to go to America without me." Her voice was tearless now, resolute.

Kien closed his eyes and saw his small family aboard the *Sea Breeze*, the fishing boat that had taken them out of Vietnam. He saw Mai feeding the old Grandfather first, even though she herself went hungry. He remembered how she had steered the boat by starlight, how she had bailed water during storms, how she had faced the cruel pirates of the South China Sea. That was Mai—uncomplaining, dependable, and so brave.

She was being brave now. His throat felt raw as he said, "We are going to stay together, Mai. I know I am not your blood brother. But before he died, your grandfather made me his adopted grandson. He made me promise to take care of you and Loc, no matter what happened. You are my family, now. We have got each other, and that's all that matters. Here . . ." He took the bag of Vietnamese sand from his shirt and put it into Mai's hands. "Hold this for me. It's a promise that everything will be all right for us!"

As Mai's fingers curled around the bag of precious sand, Kien whispered fiercely to Heaven, "We have to get to America soon. We have to!"

2

Five weeks later, they were on a plane to America.

Mai was so terrified of the huge steel machine that she could barely move a muscle once she was seated inside the plane. Loc soon forgot his awe when he discovered that his wonderful plane seat tilted back and forth at the touch of a button. As for Kien, he had never been so excited in his life.

"Mai, look!" he shouted. "Look! We are floating over the clouds!"

Mai shut her eyes tightly. "I don't want to look! Just tell me when we get to America," she begged Kien.

Kien wasn't in any hurry. He wanted to float in the blue sky for a long time. "If I stepped out of this plane, I'm sure I could walk on those clouds," he mused.

"No you couldn't. You'd fall right through and smash up on the earth," a voice said behind them. Kien turned around and saw that a young man was grinning at him. "I know how you feel, though. It would be fun to be able to grow wings and fly!"

The young man's name was Phat Dao, and he was on his way to join his uncle and aunt in Travor, California. When Kien told Phat that he and his family would be living with the Olsons in Bradley, California, Phat pulled out a road map.

"My uncle Huy sent me this map," he told Kien. "See. Here is Bradley, and here, by the sea, is Travor."

Kien was surprised. "I did not think California was such a big place!" he exclaimed.

Phat nodded. "America is a huge country," he told Kien. He also explained that, at home, he had been studying to become a lawyer before the fall of Saigon. "After the Communists came, I was sent to a 'resettlement camp' where I cut down trees and helped build houses. I wouldn't have minded this, if the Communists did not try to tell me how to think!" Phat added that he wanted to study law again, in America. "That is, if my uncle doesn't need my help. He's a fisherman, Kien. Travor is a fishing town. From what Uncle Huy says, it's a friendly place."

Would Bradley be a friendly place, too? Up to this moment, Kien had only wanted to get his family safely to America. After what had happened to poor Lam, he had been terrified that something might go wrong. Now, suddenly, he thought about the Olsons. After all, they did not really know Steve well. He had seemed friendly enough on board the ship, and his letters were pleasant, too. But how welcoming would he really be, once the Hos stepped off the plane?

The plane trip took a very long time. Mai was sick on the fatty food served at mealtime, and this started her cough again. Loc became cranky and whined and complained till he finally fell asleep. Kien was the only one wide awake when they first spotted the lights of America.

"We are here, finally!" Phat exulted. "If I know my uncle, he is at the airport waiting for me." He gave Kien a friendly smile. "I am sure the Olsons will be there for you, also."

Will they? Kien wondered. His uneasiness increased as the plane descended and finally bumped to a landing. He did not say anything to Loc or Mai, but nursed his

worries along while the immigration and customs offi-
cials checked their papers and belongings. When it was
finally over, Kien couldn't keep still any longer.

"Do you see the Olsons anywhere?" he whispered to
Mai and Loc as they left the processing area and were
led into a room where many people were waiting.

Neither of them answered. Both Mai and Loc were
dazed and a little frightened by all the bright lights, the
people. The airport was so huge . . . and the people
spoke a strange, harsh-sounding language. There was no
sign of Steve Olson or his family. They aren't here. They
haven't come to meet us, Kien thought, and his hopes
plunged.

"Kien! Mai! Loc!"

Kien jerked around. The tall young officer from the
Camelot was running toward them, followed by a fair-
haired young woman and a little boy.

"Bow!" Kien hissed to Mai and Loc. As the Olsons
hurried up, the Hos placed palm against palm and
bowed deeply. Their bows were lost in the Olsons' hugs.

"You finally got here!" Steve cried. "Your plane was
late. We were worried."

Diane said something in English, as she put an arm
around Kien and stooped to kiss Loc. Then she looked at
Mai, and her face changed. She said something to Steve.

"Diane wants to know if Mai has been sick," Steve
said to Kien. "She doesn't look well. Has she been ill?"

Suddenly, Kien was scared all over again. Mai did
look sick and weak. Could the Olsons turn them away?
Could they refuse to sponsor a sick girl? "No, she's not
sick," Kien stammered. As if sensing Kien's fear, Mai
tried to smile.

"I am just tired," she murmured. "I am well . . ."

And then her words were lost in the dreadful coughing. Kien closed his eyes. It was all over. Diane Olson
would listen to Mai's terrible cough and send them
away. He could hear dismissal in the urgent way she
spoke to Steve. Steve cleared his throat.

"Kien, Diane thinks. . . ," Steve began, then hesitated.

Kien opened his eyes and squared his shoulders. Whatever was said, he would not cry. He would not fall apart. He looked straight into Steve's face and was bewildered, for there was nothing in Olson's eyes except concern.

"Diane thinks we'd better get Mai straight home," Steve was saying, in Vietnamese. "Good food and rest will . . . Mai, why are you crying? What's the matter?"

Mai was sobbing, and the sobs, mingling with her coughs, made it impossible for her to speak. Kien explained, "She was afraid you might not accept us since she's sick."

"Might not accept—" Steve bit off the words, then turned to translate to Diane. The blond woman had tears in her own eyes as she put her arms around Mai and half cradling, half leading, began to walk away from the rest of them. "Come on, Kien, Loc," Steve Olson said. "Let's go to the car. Kien, come with me. Tad, you look after Loc."

Kien had hardly paid attention to the small blond boy who had stood silently beside his parents all this time. Now, he looked down into a round, mischievous face.

"Hi, Loc," Tad said. "Hi, Kien!" Then he grabbed Loc by the hand and started hurrying after his mother and Mai. Bewildered but willing, Loc went with Tad.

The airport was even bigger and more confusing than Kien had thought. It was filled with people and noise, and Kien's head ached. After a great deal of walking, they reached a large area filled with parked cars. So many cars, Kien thought, and all of them so big! He was impressed when Steve pointed the way to one of the larger cars.

"Here's our car, Kien," he said. "We're going home."

Diane took Mai into the back seat and held her in her arms. Loc and Tad went into the back seat too, and Kien got in front with Steve. Perhaps this was why he was the only one who realized how fast Steve Olson was driving! Zip! Steve's car shot in front of another. Zap! It overtook and passed a truck. Kien was paralyzed with fear.

"Please, Elder Brother," he stammered, "couldn't you go a bit slower?"

Steve laughed. "Look around you, Kien. Everyone is going fast. If I went more slowly, a car would probably hit me."

Kien realized that Steve was right. Everybody drove incredibly fast here in America! It was as if there were some great race going on. As he grew used to the rapid speed, Kien began to enjoy himself.

"Tell me what is wrong with Mai," Steve said. "Has she had that cough for a long time?"

"It started to get worse in the camp in Hong Kong," Kien said. For the first time in months, it was as if something tight and tense inside him was beginning to relax. He felt drowsy. "I was afraid that the doctors in the camp would not allow Mai to come to America, but they said her cough was just bronchitis."

"It must have been terrible for you! We tried to get you out of Hong Kong sooner, but there are so many refugees there that it is hard to move quickly. Diane and I contacted an agency as soon as I reached America, and they interviewed us. Then, we had to wait some time before we were told we could sponsor you. Kien? Are you listening?"

But Steve Olson was talking to himself. Kien was fast asleep.

Kien slept till they reached Bradley, many hours later. There, in the small house of many rooms, Diane put Mai to bed, soothing her cough as gently as Lam had done in the refugee camp. Kien noticed that Mai trusted Diane and turned to her for help and comfort.

Loc was in good hands, too. He and Tad had chattered to each other in the car, even though they could not understand each other's language. Now, they were communicating with signs and gestures. "It looks like they'll get on just fine." Steve smiled at Kien. "It's a good thing, since they're sharing a room." He put an arm around Kien, who was looking about him. "Do you like your new home?"

Kien nodded, speechless. To him, this house was like a palace. He had never seen so many rooms before. There was a room for eating, a room in which to sit and talk to guests, a room in which to bathe, where a turn of the tap brought hot and cold water.

"Be careful of the tap," Steve warned Kien. "You could burn yourself if the water's too hot."

But the greatest wonder in the house was his room. *My* room, Kien thought as Steve led him down a hallway from the room Loc and Tad shared, and across from Mai's room. Kien's room was smaller than the other bedrooms, but to Kien it looked enormous. There was a desk in this room, and a bed, and a chair, and a closet. Near the wall of the room was a dressing table with a mirror above it, and on top of the dressing table was a wristwatch.

"We thought you should have it, so that you could tell time in America," Steve joked, as Kien picked up the watch and held it wordlessly. When Kien could not speak even to say thanks, Steve went on, "You will need to know what time it is, Kien. After all, once you go to school—"

"School?" Kien's excitement lessened a little. "But there is no need for me to go to school, Elder Brother. I can work."

"No work for you. You've taken care of your brother and sister for a long time. Now, Diane and I want you to have a normal childhood. Besides, in America, fifteen-year-old boys have to go to school."

School, Kien thought. He had spent his life avoiding schools, and books, and learning. Then he felt cheered. Surely, there would be a way to avoid this unwanted schooling. His excitement soared again as he touched his beautiful new wristwatch and looked around his own room.

Steve Olson watched him with a smile. "Rest, now. Kien, remember, you're safe in America, now. All you need to do is to be happy!"

3

Kien woke up smelling the coffee Diane was perking in the kitchen. He yawned and glanced at the new wristwatch Steve had given him. "Six o'clock," he muttered. "Too early to get up . . ."

He was about to burrow down under the warm quilts and go back to sleep again when he heard Mai at the door.

"Kien? Are you still asleep? Don't you remember that we are supposed to go to school today for the first time?"

Kien pulled the pillow over his head. This was the day he had been dreading since their arrival in America two weeks ago. They had not been sent to school at once because Mai had been sick for many days, and Kien had hoped that the Olsons might forget the idea altogether.

"Go away," he told Mai. "I am not going anywhere."

Mai pushed the door open and stood shaking her head at him. "You lazy one," she accused. "You're not even out of bed!"

Mai was all dressed up and her dark hair had been brushed till it shone. Kien gave her a disgusted look. Trust a girl to like the idea of school! And it wasn't just

Mai who seemed happy. In the hallway, Loc and Tad were pretending they were planes.

"Why can't you mind your own business?" Kien demanded.

Mai smiled. She was still thin, but her cheeks were pink and her eyes were very bright today. "Kien," she said, "Grandfather would have wanted us to go to school, don't you think?"

Kien couldn't think of a word to say. Here in the comfortable room that was all his own, he could feel the presence of Teacher Van Chi. He had to swallow hard to get rid of the lump in his throat.

Just then, Tad, followed by Loc, came tearing into Kien's room. Loc jumped onto Kien's stomach, knocking him flat.

"I'm a rocket!" Loc yelled in English. "Bi-ig rocket!"

"Thoi dii! Enough, you little pest!" Kien spluttered.

Steve now appeared in the doorway. "You little guys get dressed and let's have breakfast," he ordered. "Come on, Mai. Let Kien get ready for school in peace."

The room emptied. Kien got up, rubbing his sore stomach. That Loc was getting heavy! Of them all, Loc was the one who liked American food the best, and he ate everything Diane cooked. Loc was ahead of them in English, too, because he and Tad were forever gabbling together in a mixed-up half-English, half-Vietnamese language of their own. Mai had also picked up many English words from Diane during the long hours Diane had nursed her back to health. But Kien . . .

"I hate this English," Kien muttered to himself. It was a slippery, pesty language that just wouldn't wind itself around his tongue. It was a lucky thing that Steve could speak Vietnamese and had been able to get shore duty so that he could stay with his new Vietnamese family!

Kien got out of bed and went across the hall to the bathroom for his morning wash. The water scalded him when he turned it on. It was not going to be a good day.

He hurried through his washing and then went back to his room to dress. "Good morning," he said in English to his reflection in the mirror over his dresser. "My name is Kien."

A burst of laughter interrupted him. Tad and Loc were peering in the doorway. "Kien's making funny faces!" Tad screamed.

Kien chased the two brats down the hall and into the kitchen, where the others were already seated around the breakfast table. Kien sat next to Mai, as usual. He was still uncomfortable with the knife and fork and spoon that were placed by his plate, and this morning he dropped his fork twice before he could eat the eggs Diane slid onto his plate. School, he thought. Ugh!

Mai's eyes were shining. "I want to learn," Mai said in English to Diane. "I go . . . school, learn talk . . . you."

Diane hugged Mai. Kien, watching them, felt a small twinge of jealousy. Mai and Diane had grown so close! Mai is certainly her favorite, Kien thought, and then had to admit that Diane was nice to them all. She fussed around Loc, mothering him just as she did Tad, and she was always trying to get Kien to like American food. Since Kien liked the chocolate-chip brownies Diane baked, she would often bake a batch especially for him. Still, Mai was the favorite. He bit into his tasteless eggs and sighed.

Steve heard the sigh and smiled. "Cheer up, Kien. School might not be so bad. Give it a chance!" He glanced at the kitchen clock. "Almost time to go. Normally, you would take a bus to school, but today I am driving you there in the car. I want to introduce you to Mr. Varney, the principal of Farrell High School."

Usually Kien loved to drive in Steve's big car. Now that he was used to speeding cars, he enjoyed the feel of the powerful engine whooshing under him. Today, he hoped Steve would drive slowly.

Steve did not drive slowly enough. Kien sighed again when he saw the American school. It was huge and surrounded by large grassy fields. Steve explained that students of the high school played sports on the fields.

"Maybe you'll go in for sports, Kien," Steve said. "I

played baseball and football when I was in high school."

"I do not know how the games are played," Kien muttered.

A group of boys and girls were drifting toward the big school. Kien looked them over, thinking that they were all bigger than Mai and himself. The Americans looked at the newcomers curiously, and one of them, a boy about Kien's age, smiled and waved. Kien wanted to wave back, but was too nervous.

Mai was looking nervous, too. "It's a big school, Kien!" she whispered. "I am afraid we'll get lost!"

Steve now led them into the school building to meet Mr. Varney. The principal was a small, plump man who shook Mai's and Kien's hands as he welcomed them. He then spoke with Steve, who looked serious and nodded many times.

"What's wrong?" Kien whispered when the talking was over.

Steve reassured him. "Nothing is wrong, Kien. Mr. Varney suggested that I leave you here for an hour or so." He smiled at the look on Kien's and Mai's faces. "Now, don't worry. He just wants to show you around the school and introduce you to your teachers. Tomorrow you'll start regular classes. Okay?"

Not okay at all! Kien wanted to protest, but Steve was already walking away. Now Mr. Varney began to talk. With gestures he explained that Mai and Kien were to come into his office, sit down and wait.

"Perhaps they are deciding what we must learn here," Mai whispered. Kien nodded glumly. How are we going to learn anything when we can't understand English? he wondered.

After some time, the principal beckoned to Mai and Kien. He led them down a long corridor flanked on both sides by classrooms. Through windows in the classroom doors, Kien and Mai could see students at their desks. Many were studying, but a few looked to be asleep, others were talking behind their teacher's back, and a few were throwing things at each other. Mai was shocked.

"Grandfather would never have allowed that!" she gasped.

Mr. Varney now stopped at a door. He knocked on the door and a young, skinny man with a drooping brown mustache came to the door. The principal pointed a finger at this young man and said: "Mis-ter Hun-ter. Your tutor."

"What is a 'tutor'?" Mai asked Kien, who shrugged. Then, he nearly jumped out of his skin as Mr. Hunter spoke in a deep, firm voice.

"Mai, Kien," Mr. Hunter said. *"Tieng chao buoi sang."*

Mai's mouth fell open and Kien stammered, "G-good morning, *Thay* Hunter! Then you speak Vietnamese?"

The teacher shook his head as if to say, "That is all I know." Then, he leaned forward to touch both their shoulders before tapping himself on the chest. He spoke in English, but Kien knew that he was saying, "We will learn from each other." For the first time since school had been mentioned, Kien felt a little better.

But the good feeling did not last. Mr. Varney confused them thoroughly by taking them to many classrooms, introducing them to many teachers. And since Mai was younger than Kien, it seemed she had to have different teachers. Kien's head began to whirl. How would they possibly be able to remember all these teachers? Mai looked ready to cry.

But Mr. Varney had understood their confusion. In one of the classrooms they visited, the principal introduced Kien and Mai to two American students called Bob and Alyssa. He explained through gestures that Bob and Alyssa would act as guides around school and help the Vietnamese make friends. Alyssa only smiled shyly at Mai, but Kien recognized Bob as the boy who had waved at him outside the school earlier that morning.

"He-lo," he said in English, and Bob grinned widely.

"Hi, Kien," he said and winked in a friendly way.

Thankfully, this was the last stop of their tour around the big school. Kien was relieved when he saw Steve waiting for them. Though he and Mai waited patiently till Steve had spoken with their principal, they began to talk almost as soon as they were out of Mr. Varney's office.

"This school is so big!" Mai cried. "Kien and I are in separate classes. I will get lost . . ."

"It is a waste of time," Kien protested. "I can't understand one word these Americans are saying. I should not be in this school, Elder Brother. I should be at work!"

"*Nung lai!* Stop!" Steve put his hands over his ears. "If you talk so much in school, they will throw you out!"

Mai shook her head. "No, they won't. In one classroom I saw students talking while their teacher looked straight at them! I actually saw a boy put his feet up on his desk!" Her eyes were shocked. "School is different here. *Everything* is different here!"

Kien nodded gloomily. "That much is for sure," he said.

4

Kien decided that he didn't want to ride the school bus home. He needed to move, to walk, to free himself for a little while from this cage called school, which closed around him each morning at eight and kept him trapped at a desk until two. For several months he had endured this, and today he felt ready to burst.

"I walking home," he told his friend Bob. "You tell Mai?"

Bob nodded. "Sure, Kien. But don't you want to come downtown with us? There's a new kid in school and some of us are going to take the bus downtown. We're taking Sim to Abbott's for pizza."

"Maybe later," Kien said.

One good thing about all this school was that he could now speak enough English to make people understand him. Of course, his English wasn't as good as Mai's. Mai was always studying, her nose buried in a book.

Kien shifted his books under his arm and began to walk. It was a beautiful May afternoon. All during school Kien had longed to run out of the classroom, race out the door, disappear into this warm golden day. He had shuffled and shifted so much that his tutor, Mr. Hunter, had shaken his head.

"Restless, Kien?" he had asked, whispy mustaches

23

rumpling into a smile. "I know how you feel, but we have to study first."

Kien had tried to keep his mind on his work. He didn't mind studying with Mr. Hunter, who worked so patiently, teaching both Mai and Kien through games and special lessons. It was due to Mr. Hunter that Kien could speak English at all, and it was Mr. Hunter who told exciting stories about brave ships' captains and Vikings and noble American Indians. As for the rest of the school day, it wasn't worth too much!

Besides, it was terribly confusing. At times Kien couldn't make any sense out of school or his American classmates. Take this morning, for instance. It had started out, as usual, with a "homeroom" during which a teacher recorded the absences of the day. Before homeroom began, Bob had been helping Kien go over a history lesson that told about America's breaking away from the English king. Bob seemed quite proud of the old patriots who framed the new America's Constitution.

Yet, when Mr. Varney's voice came over the intercom inviting students to rise and salute the American flag, hardly anyone in the class got up! Most of the students, including Bob, sat where they were. They yawned, looked bored, or talked among themselves.

Kien had asked Bob to explain this. "Why not stand for flag?" he had asked. He couldn't understand Bob's explanation that in America nobody could *make* students salute the flag. "It's in the Constitution," Bob had said.

That was just one puzzling thing. Kien couldn't understand other things about the school, including the school rules. This school had so many rules that the office had to print a handbook full of do's and don'ts. Each student was given a copy lest anybody forget what to do or not to do! And, in case there were not enough rules, there were passes. You had to have a pass to go from one place to another, including the bathroom!

In spite of the rules and passes, however, Kien noticed that students were often rude to their teachers or openly disrupted a class. When this happened, the students were given "detention," which was not really a punishment at all. Did it make any sense to have all those rules with nothing to back them up? Kien shook his head over it all.

However, the worst thing, the very worst thing about school, was that it was keeping him from doing things he really wanted to do. Ever since Mr. Hunter had shown him slides and filmstrips of America, Kien wanted to explore this new country.

"I want to see what a desert looks like," Kien muttered out loud as he walked. "I would like to see a cactus as tall as many men. I want to ride down an angry river. But because of this stupid school I cannot do as I . . ."

The school bus swooped by him with a whoosh of sound. Kien saw Bob wave from one window and thought he spotted Mai in the back of the bus between two of her friends. Mai did not bother to wave at him. Kien couldn't understand what had happened to Mai lately. She not only liked this school, but she was making many friends with whom she talked for hours on the telephone. Either that . . . or she was talking to Diane. Those two always had their heads together. Once, Kien had commented on this, and Mai looked surprised.

"But, Kien, she's teaching me so many new things," she had said. "We're in America, and we have to learn how things are done here."

Kien drew a lungful of California air and tried to forget about school, and Mai, too! He wanted to think of things that made him feel happy. He liked California, and he liked this town of Bradley. He enjoyed the Olsons' neighbors, who were always friendly and hired him to do odd jobs. He liked the money those odd jobs brought him. Kien walked along, feeling the frustrations of the school day drain away from him.

When he came to the road that would lead him back to the Olsons' home, he hesitated. Do I really want to go back right away? he asked himself. He decided to walk

some more. He would just see where this other street
led.

It led to another street, and that street led to a road
called Bear's Paw Road that wound around and around.
Kien walked along, enjoying himself, and was surprised
when he ended up in the center of town. Kien looked
around, pleased with himself. So this was how one
walked to town! There was the post office, there the fire
department, there the bus terminal. There were also
many shops full of interesting things. Kien began to
think of all the things he would like to buy for himself
someday. The dollars he got from odd jobs might buy a
small radio . . . or a new pair of jeans. It would feel
good to buy his own clothes.

"Hey, Kien."

Surprised, Kien turned and saw Bob waving to him
from across the street. A group of high school students
were with him. "Hey, Kien, you're late!" Bob called.
"We just finished having our pizza. Want to join us for
ice cream?"

Kien's stomach growled at the thought of food. He
glanced at his watch. It was nearly five o'clock! Had he
really been walking around for three hours? No wonder
he was hungry!

"I'm coming!" he called and began to walk over to join
the others. As he walked, he spotted a stranger in the
group, a boy with bright-red hair and broad shoulders.
This boy was staring at Kien in an unfriendly way, and,
as Kien drew closer, said something to the rest of the
group in a derisive tone.

Kien could not hear what this red-haired boy said, but
Bob looked surprised. "Kien? He's a good kid!" Bob protested. "Hey, Kien, come meet Sim Evans. He's the new
kid I told you about. His dad just got a job here in
Bradley."

"Hi," Kien said, but instead of replying, the redheaded boy turned away from Kien and spat on the
pavement. He began to walk away. After a few seconds,
the others followed. Kien stopped, unsure. Should he go

with them or not? He glanced at Bob for guidance. "Bob?" he asked uncertainly.

Bob's cheeks were bright pink. He glanced after the others, then at Kien. "Don't mind Sim," he muttered. "He's new. He doesn't understand."

"Are you coming, Bob?" the redheaded boy called. "You with us, or what?"

Bob looked down at the pavement. "I'll see you at school tomorrow, Kien," he mumbled.

"Okay. Sure. . . ," but Bob did not wait to hear what Kien had to say. He was hurrying after Sim Evans and the others. Kien stood where he was, feeling a little lost. He wished that Bob would turn around and wave, ask him to join them.

"Kien! Where have you been?"

He turned around, staring. Diane, in Steve's car, was waving to him from the curb. What was she doing here? And why was she looking so angry? As Kien ran to the car, Diane cried, "I've been looking all over for you!"

Kien blinked. "You look . . . me?"

"School let out hours ago!" Diane was very angry. She motioned Kien into the car and added crossly, "When you didn't get home, Mai explained that you were walking. I expected you to be home within the hour. Where have you been?"

Kien couldn't understand why Diane was angry. "Not good I walk?"

Diane stared at him, opened her mouth to speak, then shook her head. "You don't understand, do you? Kien, I was worried." Seeing that he still couldn't understand, she sighed and started the car. "Oh, never mind. Kien, you think so differently from Mai and Loc. Why is that?"

Kien said nothing. The strange, lost feeling that had begun when Bob turned his back on him was stronger now. He was silent as Diane drove back to the Olsons' home, and when she parked the car he got out without a word and carried his schoolbooks into the house. He could hear Loc and Tad playing someplace, and in the kitchen Mai was on the phone.

"Talking to your friends again," Kien snapped, glad to be able to scold someone. "Women!"

"We're doing our homework," Mai explained, hurt. "Why are you in such a bad temper? And where have you been?"

Kien went into his room and slammed the door. He set his books down on the desk. Homework . . . I should do that too, he thought dismally, but he made no move to open his books. Why? he asked himself. Why can't I be like Mai, like Loc? They are happy here. They like school. Why can't I just settle down?

He sat down at his desk and opened his books and tried to concentrate, but his mind would not stay on his lessons. Instead, his mind filled with images—snow-capped mountains and raging rivers and tall cacti growing in hot, dry deserts. He thought of the oceans, too—oceans where people fished and went to sea in boats. Suddenly, he remembered Phat Dao, the young man he had met on the plane. I wonder if Phat is happy. I wonder how he is doing in Travor.

There was a knock on the door. "Can I come in?" Steve asked, in the doorway. "I'd like to talk to you, Kien."

Steve looked serious as he came to sit on the edge of Kien's bed. Kien felt uncomfortable. "I am in trouble?" he asked, in English.

"Not really. But, Kien, you just can't disappear without telling anyone as you did today. Diane was worried."

"Why, worried?" Kien lapsed into rapid Vietnamese. "Elder Brother, I don't understand. I walked all over Vietnam during the war. I was on a boat that sailed right across the South China Sea. Storms . . . sharks . . . pirates . . . people who didn't want us to land . . . I lived through them all. After our grandfather died on the voyage, I managed to keep Mai and Loc alive. And, in the refugee camp, I worked in the city to buy Mai's medicine." He paused. "Why does Diane worry if I walk in the town?"

Steve looked embarrassed. "You're new here. You could have lost your way."

"If that had happened," Kien said patiently, "I would have gone to a place with a telephone. As you taught me when I first came to America, I would put the smallest silver coin in the slot of the phone, and dial 891-9171. Is that not correct?"

Steve began to laugh. "You are correct, Younger Brother," he said. "I see there is no reason to worry about your safety. But, Kien," he added in English now, "there are rules."

Kien scowled at the word.

"You see, each of us knows where the others are at all times. That way, no one needs to worry. Next time you go someplace, just *tell* one of us. That's all!"

Kien nodded slowly. "I tell."

"Good!" Steve reached out to pat Kien's shoulder. "Diane's not angry with you. In fact, she's out there baking a batch of those chocolate-chip brownies you like!"

When Steve had gone, Kien closed his books and stacked them on his desk. He stared past the stack of books toward a window that looked into the backyard. Outside, twilight was turning everything gray, and in that grayness Tad shouted at Loc.

"Loc! Hey, Loc! What'll we play now?"

"Hide-and-seek? How about hide-and-seek?"

"*Tuy ong.* As you like, Loc! I'll be 'it' first. One, two, three . . ."

In the kitchen, Mai laughed. Kien thought, Loc loves it here. Mai is happy here.

"It's not so bad," he said out loud. "I like Mr. Hunter, and Steve is a good man. Diane makes those brownies just for me. And Bob is my friend . . ."

Then he stopped, remembering the big redheaded boy who had spat so contemptuously onto the ground. He remembered the way Bob had gone off with Sim Evans and the others.

Kien drew a long breath and let it out slowly. For the first time in a long while, he felt all alone.

5

Kien didn't want to go to school the next morning, but he could not convince Diane that he was sick. "You look fine," Diane told him. "Don't get into the habit of skipping school, Kien."

Kien felt sorry for himself as he got onto the bus. When Mai tried to cheer him up, he snapped at her. "Go off with your own friends and leave me alone!" he growled. When he saw Bob at school, he didn't walk over to say hello. After a moment, however, Bob joined Kien.

"Hi," he smiled.

Kien didn't smile back. "Why you go away so fast yesterday?" he demanded.

Bob looked flustered. "I didn't go off anywhere 'so fast.' What are you mad about?"

Before Kien could answer, a loud voice called, "Bob! C'mover here! I have to tell you something!"

Kien looked toward this new speaker and saw the big redheaded boy, Sim Evans. He saw the way Sim's eyes flickered over him and then moved away. Insolently. Contemptuously. "What is wrong with that boy?" Kien asked Bob.

Bob shifted his feet. "Oh . . . he's okay. He just moved from Southern California, you know. His dad—"

"Bob, you coming, or what?"

Bob hesitated, then moved off with a rapid, "See you, Kien!"

Kien said nothing. He watched his friend Bob walk over to join the crowd of youths around big Sim Evans, then he started to walk away in the opposite direction. Something made him look back over his shoulder, and it was then he saw the look in the redhead's eyes. Sim's dark eyes were angry and hating. Kien had seen eyes like that before, during his wanderings on the South China Sea.

Why should Sim dislike me? Kien wondered, bewildered. I don't even know him! Now, he heard Sim Evans say in a loud voice, "All gooks are no good! You ask my father. He should know! Look at the way those gooks treated him!"

"Gooks?" Kien wondered. What were "gooks"?

He asked Mr. Hunter this, later that day. The tutor gave Kien a level look. "Has anyone called you that, Kien?"

"I not sure," Kien replied truthfully. "New boy . . . Sim Evans . . . say gook no good. What means this 'gook'?"

Mr. Hunter's eyes were angry as he replied, "It is a slang word, a very rude and stupid word. Some people use it to mean 'Vietnamese.'" Kien's eyes narrowed. "Kien, if this Sim Evans insulted you, you must tell Mr. Varney. We don't allow that kind of nonsense here at Farrell!"

Kien thought about it, then shook his head. "First," he explained, "I want know why boy hates me." Perhaps Sim had Kien confused with another Vietnamese boy. "I ask Bob," he told Mr. Hunter.

Getting Bob alone wasn't easy. He seemed to have attached himself to the growing number of boys who followed Sim around. By listening, Kien discovered that Sim was very good at playing games and was a football linebacker, whatever that meant. Perhaps this was why

Bob looked uncomfortable when Kien pulled him aside just before lunch.

"I want question," Kien said sternly. "Why is Sim Evans hating me, calling me gook?"

Bob looked terribly uncomfortable. "He doesn't hate *you*, Kien, not really. I guess his father worked in a plant in Southern Calfornia—"

A plant? He would never understand this language. "He is gardener?"

Bob grinned and looked more like his usual self. "No. He worked in a factory. I guess some Vietnamese people came and worked for less money at the same factory and Sim's father lost his job."

Kien understood. "So because father loses work, he calling all Vietnamese gook. Is stupid. Nothing to do with me."

"I know that. Listen, he's new, Kien. I'll set him straight," Bob promised.

They walked together into the lunchroom. Kien wondered if Bob would really set Sim Evans "straight." Though Bob was smaller than most boys his age, he loved football and other games. Would he dare to speak frankly to big Sim?

"I told him you were okay," Bob was saying as he and Kien joined the lunch line. "I told him not to pick on you, but—"

There was a snicker just behind Kien. He glanced over his shoulder and saw Sim Evans standing there, surrounded by a group of youths who were as big as he was. These were boys from the varsity football team, Bob whispered to Kien. Sim grinned at Bob.

"Hey, Bob, I thought you were an okay kid. You're not a gook lover, are you?"

"Don't pay any attention!" Bob said, but his face went beet red. Kien felt anger building up inside him.

"Hey, Gook, you talkee English? Vietnamese are so stupid, man! Can't teach them anything! They're like monkeys!" Sim made monkey sounds, scratching his armpits. Kien's anger nearly choked him. He thought of

Teacher Van Chi and his pride in Vietnam and its people. He thought of the small bag of Vietnamese sand waiting in his drawer at the Olson house. He wanted to turn around and hit Sim Evans, but prudence kept him where he was.

Just then, Mr. Varney walked into the lunchroom and Sim stopped taunting Kien. Kien walked blindly through the lunch line, not caring what was put on his tray. Once seated at a table, he could not bear to eat. His appetite was gone, and only the sour anger remained, flooding his stomach and throat.

Bob came up to Kien's table and banged his lunch tray down next to Kien's. "Don't worry about what that Sim says," he told Kien angrily. "He's not worth bothering about. I . . . I didn't know what a jerk he was."

It was an apology, and Kien nodded, trying to smile. Bob's loyalty should have made him feel better, but somehow it did not. All he could think of was Sim, and his terrible, mocking words and gestures. Supposing Sim teases Mai like that? Kien worried.

But Mai was in a lower class, and she was a girl . . . not a small, scrawny, weak-looking Vietnamese boy. Perhaps because Kien looked so easy to pick on, Sim Evans spent most of his free school time devising ways to make him miserable. This made school even more unbearable for Kien. Those students who had accepted him as a friend till now either avoided him or openly drifted into Sim Evans' camp. Many, egged on by Evans, teased Kien openly.

One day, during study hall, Sim shoved something in front of Kien. It was a page torn from a magazine, and over it Sim had scrawled: "Gook, go back to the jungle!"

Kien flushed. He didn't have to take this. He would stuff the magazine page down the big redhead's throat! He almost got out of his seat to do this, then realized that he was looking at a photograph that was somehow familiar. There were docks, and fishing boats, and a group of smiling Vietnamese men and women and children. Underneath the photo was the caption: "Vietnamese make Travor their home!"

"Travor," Kien breathed. That was where Phat Dao had been going! He forgot about Sim Evans as he began to read the article. Some of the words were too difficult for him, but he understood that in Travor, California, a group of Vietnamese refugees had settled down to fish and prosper. There was a map showing Travor's location, and more photos of happy Vietnamese at work and play. Surely, Kien thought, in Travor no one would call him "gook."

He went home from school that day feeling thoughtful. Travor—the name of the town stuck in his mind and refused to leave. He was still thinking about Travor when he walked into the Olson kitchen. Diane saw his face and raised her eyebrows.

"Bad day, Kien?" she asked.

"Is okay." But Diane was not fooled.

"Something is bothering you," she said. She came over to Kien, and put a hand on his shoulder. "Can you tell me about it?"

Kien wished he could. Mai confided so easily in Diane, and Loc was already calling her "Mama" like little Tad. Kien wanted to explain his feelings to Diane, but at the same time something made him stand aloof, made him tense ever so slightly under the friendly pressure of her hand. Sensing this, Diane moved away.

"Mrs. Landon, next door, wants you to mow her lawn," she said in a matter-of-fact voice. She smiled at Kien as if nothing was wrong, but Kien knew he puzzled Diane, worried her.

He took some of his frustrations out on the Landon lawn, mowing it within an inch of its life. When he returned to the Olsons', the kitchen had a heavenly smell. Diane was not there, but a huge plate of chocolate-chip brownies sat at Kien's place at table. There was also a note that said: "Cheer up! Whatever it is, things will get better. Diane."

The brownies tasted wonderful, and Kien did feel

cheered for a while. But things did not get better. Instead, they got progressively worse. In the next few days Sim Evans taunted Kien at every chance, tripped him, knocked his books from his hands, made crude remarks about "slant eyes" and "gooks." Sim was clever, too. He never did this in front of a teacher or school aide. Finally, Kien was desperate. He asked Mai what he should do.

"Tell the principal, as Mr. Hunter said," Mai advised. Kien shook his head. "Then ignore him! A person like that is not worth worrying about."

"How can I ignore someone who follows me, crashes into me, insults me?" Kien demanded indignantly. "Mai, you aren't paying attention!"

Mai was embarrassed. Then she laughed. "Oh, Kien, I'm sorry. You see, I'm planning my party."

Kien stared. "Your what?"

"My very first party!" Mai's eyes glowed with excitement. "Diane says that every girl should have a party, and she is going to help me have one. I'm inviting Alyssa and Jean and other girls, too, and we'll listen to records and eat ice cream."

Kien said nothing more. Mai was more concerned about her stupid girls party than about his very real problem with Sim! He was sorry he had said anything to Mai. Now he felt worse than before.

The next day, during gym, things came to a head. Kien had come to the gym a few moments early. The gym teacher was not yet there, so Kien began bouncing a basketball on the gym floor. Suddenly, a sneering voice behind him said, "Stop that noise, you stupid slant-eye!"

Kien turned and saw Sim standing there, hands on hips, red head cocked to one side. The rest of the gym class was coming in, and the others plainly heard Sim say, "You make me sick to my stomach, Gook boy. Your ancestors hung from trees like apes. Ape face! You aren't even human!"

Kien threw the ball he was holding right at Sim. It hit

the big boy in the chest and bounced off. "You stop!" Kien yelled. "Right now, stop! Who you, talking ape? You like monkey too. Red-hair monkey with ugly face!"

Sim turned brick red. "Why, you little . . ."

Kien wished he could insult Sim in Vietnamese. The English words were so strange and clumsy. "You think we stupid? We not stupid. You are! Stupid! Stupid!"

Sim lunged for Kien. "Fight!" Kien heard someone yell.

Kien's heart was hammering. For a big boy, Sim was very swift. Kien barely managed to sidestep Sim's lunge. Then he found himself caught by two huge, viselike hands. He punched at Sim's midsection, nearly breaking his fist. "Now, I'll show you, you little punk!" Sim snarled.

"Break this up! What's going on here?" The gym teacher had arrived. Sim let go of Kien.

"He started it!" Sim shouted. "Ask anyone!"

To Kien's great surprise, a boy spoke up. "That's not true. Sim was calling Kien names. Kien had enough. Sim threw the first punch."

They were sent down to the principal's office. There, Mr. Varney listened to what both boys had to say and then asked Mr. Hunter to step down to the office. Kien's tutor gave Sim Evans a cold look. "This boy has been spoiling for a fight ever since he came here," he told Mr. Varney. "He's called Kien names and tormented him. I advised Kien to tell you this before, but he wanted to handle things his own way."

Mr. Varney looked stern. "We don't tolerate that sort of behavior here, Sim. You're suspended for five days."

"What about him?" Kien had never seen such hatred as he now saw reflected in the redhead's eyes. "He gets off free, right? That's the way gooks do—"

"Get out of here before you get into more trouble!" Mr. Varney ordered. Sim said nothing more, but his look at Kien made Kien shudder.

Mr. Hunter saw that shiver. "Do you feel all right?"

he asked Kien. "Can you go back to gym class? I'll walk with you."

"You needn't worry about Sim Evans bothering you again," Mr. Varney added. "We won't stand for his kind of behavior here. You remember that, Kien!"

Kien nodded, but he didn't agree with the principal. He knew what that look in Sim Evans' eyes meant.

It meant trouble.

6

Kien was surprised when he returned to the gym. Many of the boys who had been teasing him along with Sim Evans now wanted to make friends. Others openly admired Kien for the way he had stood up to the big redhead.

"Kien's a lot smaller than Sim, but he was sick of Sim's lip," Bob said, proud of his friend. Kien found himself more popular than he had ever been.

At the Olson home, there was another burst of reaction. "He hit you?" Diane was horrified. "I am going to call up this bully's parents and tell them to leave you alone. The idea! You've suffered quite enough without Sim Evans!"

Kien felt uncomfortable. "Is okay," he protested. "I okay."

Steve dropped a hand on Kien's shoulder. "Diane, maybe we'd better let Kien handle his own battles," he said. Kien noted that Steve's voice was proud.

The little boys were interested in the fight. "Tell us how you beat up the bully," Loc begged, and Tad said that it was more interesting than stories on the television.

"On TV nobody really gets hurt," Mai pointed out. She put ice on the bruises Sim had left on Kien's arms. "That Sim is a bully and nobody really likes him at

school," she told Kien. "You were brave to fight him,
Elder Brother."

All this attention was flattering. Kien felt good enough
to tease Mai about her party. "I don't know anything
about a lot of giggling girls," he told Mai, "but if you
like, I'll help. What do you want me to do?"

Mai was delighted. "Could you get the ice cream for
me, Kien? The ice-cream store is not far from school. Diane was going to get it, but—"

"It would be a big help if Kien picked it up on his
way home from school," Diane said, when Kien's offer
had been translated to her. Her eyes were warm as she
smiled at Kien, and, for the first time since his arrival in
America, Kien felt a moment of complete belonging and
content.

Kien carried the good feelings to bed with him that
night, and they crept through his dreams, making him
wake up happier than he had been for many months.
School was almost enjoyable without the hulking
presence of Sim Evans, and everyone seemed to want to
make friends. Bob looked proud to be with Kien, and
volunteered to help him pick up Mai's ice cream after
school.

They were carrying big tubs of the ice cream down
the road when Bob suddenly said, "Uh, oh. Look, Kien.
Trouble!"

Sim Evans was sitting on the sidewalk, waiting for
them. The sun glinted in his red hair and even at a distance Kien could see the gleam in Sim's hating eyes.

"Let's turn around," Bob said nervously. "He's probably waiting for you. If we go back to the store, we could
call my folks, and . . ."

His voice died away as he looked over his shoulder.
Kien looked, too. Two big boys, both friends of Sim's,
were standing a few yards behind them, cutting off escape. Kien's hands tightened around the tub of ice
cream he was holding. His heart began to pound as Sim
drawled, "Having a party, Slant-eye?"

Kien said nothing, but icy perspiration began to slide

down his spine. Sim glanced at Bob and said contemptuously, "Get lost. We don't want you."

Bob was shaking, but he stayed where he was. "You're a bully, Sim! If you try to hurt us, you'll be in big trouble!"

Sim began to laugh. "*Try* to hurt you? No way. We're *going* to hurt you. I heard you were going to pick up that ice cream, so me and my friends have been waiting for you. We'll have a little talk, Gook. We didn't finish what you started yesterday."

"I don't talk you," Kien mumbled. He shot a glance over his shoulder, saw that Sim's friends were moving closer.

"Yeah? Well, you'd better listen good, Slant-eye." Redness was washing into Sim's face. "By the time I finish with you, you're gonna want to run straight back to your uncle Ho Chi Minh!"

Where to go? Where to run? How to get away? They would hurt him . . . hurt him badly. Kien saw sunlight glimmer dully on something one of Sim's friends held—a piece of metal pipe. They will beat me with that, Kien thought. He tried to pull himself together and to think, but his brain was like a jumbled jigsaw puzzle, and he could not get his thoughts together. Beside him, Bob whispered, "How do we get out of this, Kien?"

Then one of Sim's friends began to laugh, and for some reason this sound cut through the panic in Kien's mind. It seemed to him that he was no longer in America, but in wartime Saigon. He was being cornered by some street toughs who wanted to take away the food he had begged that day. They would kill him, unless he got away.

And suddenly, Kien was quite calm. His body continued to tremble, but he could think clearly again. I have to keep Sim talking, he thought. "I don't do anything to you," he whined, in his old street-beggar voice. "Why want to hurt me? I poor boy . . ."

Sim guffawed. "Told you he didn't have any guts. Lookit him shake!" he crowed.

"I not understanding. Please leave me alone . . ." Kien fell to his knees imploringly. But as he begged, his fingers scrabbled desperately in the dust of the road for some weapon, for something sharp. His hand closed around a stone with a jagged point—a heavy stone that fitted into the palm of his hand.

"Him and his kind," Sim jeered, as he approached, "making honest Americans lose their jobs. I'll make you pay! You're in trouble now, boy!"

"Not hurt, please!" Kien begged.

Bob was staring at Kien disgustedly, so Kien knew he was doing a good job of acting. And it wasn't just acting, either. Sim really looked mean!

Sim bent over leisurely to grab his victim. "Oh, I won't hurt you so much—" he began, and that was when Kien leaped up, the stone upraised.

"Bob, run!" he screamed.

Sim screamed, too, and staggered back, clutching his eye. "My eye . . . my eye! He hit me right in the eye!" He shouted and howled in pain, and as his friends ran to his aid, Kien and Bob fled. Within seconds, they had torn past Sim and were pelting down the road. Behind them, they could hear Sim screaming. Bob glanced over his shoulder and turned a white face toward Kien.

"You got him right in the eye!" Bob panted.

"Is old trick," Kien replied grimly. "Hit in eye . . . a man stop." It was street fighting, survival fighting, and he didn't have time to explain it to Bob. "You go home," he ordered. "If Sim and friends come, much trouble. Better we go to own house."

They parted wordlessly, each running hard. Kien raced along, his lungs searing and his heart banging against a stitch in his side. At any moment, he expected to hear Sim's friends in pursuit. Only when he came to the Olsons' street did he slow down to look over his shoulder. No one was following him. He was safe.

But not safe, either! There was Mai, standing on the front steps, the expectant smile dying on her lips as she saw Kien hurrying down the walk. "Kien!" she ex-

claimed. "You're late! Did you forget the ice cream?"
She took a closer look at him, and her eyes widened.
"What has happened?" she whispered.

Kien did not stop to explain. He pushed past her and
ran into his room and slammed the door tight shut. Then
he stood against the door, trembling all over. Reaction
had set in and his legs felt like rubber. He could see the
big boys in his mind's eye, the hating eyes, and the
metal pipe held in a powerful hand. If they had caught
him . . .

"Kien?" Mai was saying from the hallway. Her tone
was irritated. "Kien, what is it? Why did you say you'd
bring the ice cream and then forget? Now Diane has to
go get it."

"Go away . . . leave me be!" Kien muttered. All he
wanted, right now, was to be left alone.

After a while, Mai's footsteps went away. Kien felt exhausted suddenly. He lurched forward, and fell onto his
bed. I will just rest for a moment, he thought. Then, I
must think. If Sim comes here, I must be prepared.

He must have dozed off, because the next thing he
knew was that Diane was shaking him. Diane's eyebrows were pulled together in a worried frown. "Kien,"
she was saying. "Kien, wake up!"

Kien sat up, feeling a little dizzy. "What is happen?"
he muttered.

"Kien, there is a policeman here. Mr. Evans is here,
too. He says that you hurt his son, Sim, very badly."

The police! Sim's father! Blood drained away from
Kien's face. There was a roaring sound in his ears.

"Where is that boy?" a loud, booming voice now
shouted from the hallway. Kien shuddered. "I want to
see the little brute who hurt my son!"

Diane caught her lower lip in her teeth. "Did you hurt
Sim Evans?" she asked Kien. Kien nodded slowly.
"Why? Oh, Kien . . . why?"

"He come after me," Kien tried to explain, but Mai
came running into Kien's room now. Her eyes were full
of tears.

"That man is screaming and yelling and frightening my friends," she wailed. "What is happening?"

Diane put an arm around Mai. "I've telephoned Steve. He's coming home. Maybe you'd better stay right here till he comes, Kien."

"If that little creep doesn't come out, I'm coming to get him!" Mr. Evans roared.

Kien got to his feet. He felt dizzy again, but he walked toward the door. "Don't go out there, Kien. . . ," Diane began, but Kien was in the hallway and walking toward the front door. He saw Mai's friends peeping out of Mai's room, their faces white and scared. Then he looked down the hallway to where a policeman stood beside a huge, bullnecked man. The man had Sim's hating eyes.

"You!" the man shouted. He started to move toward Kien, but was restrained by the policeman.

"Mr. Evans, you stay right where you are," the policeman ordered.

The big man glared at Kien. "All right, Officer. But I'm telling you, that boy is going to jail. Hear me, you? You're going to jail! You put my Sim in the hospital, bashed his eye with a rock. You nearly put out my boy's eye with your dirty, rock-throwing gook tricks!"

"Sim come after me. . . ," Kien began. His voice sounded small and shaky.

"Liar!" Mr. Evans roared. "Slant-eyed liar!"

Now Diane, her own eyes blazing, pushed herself in front of Kien. "How dare you speak like that? Your son caused all the trouble. He picked a fight with Kien—"

Mr. Evans sneered at Diane. "I'm not talking with you. I don't talk to any gook-loving freaks!"

Just then, Steve Olson walked through the door. He was obviously angry, yet his voice was calm as he asked the policeman what was going on.

"That's what we're trying to find out," the police officer replied. "Mr. Evans is accusing this boy, Kien Ho, of assaulting his son and hurting his boy's eye."

"What happened, Kien?" Steve asked Kien.

"Sim and his friends—two friends—wait for me," Kien began. Then he cried in Vietnamese, "Elder Brother, Bob and I were bringing the ice cream home when Sim and his two friends met us. They told Bob to leave, but he stayed with me. I saw that one of Sim's friends had a metal pipe, and they said they would hurt us. So, I pretended to ask for mercy on my knees, and I found a sharp stone and hit Sim in the eye with it."

"You aimed for the eye? Why, Kien?"

"It is the most vulnerable part of the face," Kien explained. "Sim was too big for me. I had to hurt him that way."

Steve turned to the policeman and Mr. Evans and told them what Kien had said. "There was another boy there?" the policeman asked. "Can he substantiate Kien's story?"

"He'd lie!" Mr. Evans objected. "Gook lovers always lie."

Steve now lost his temper. "You shut your foul mouth!" he roared at Mr. Evans. "You look at Kien, and then tell me how that small youngster could fight a big brute like your son! Your bullyboy probably got what he deserved!"

Mr. Evans sprang forward to hit Steve. The policeman got in between them. "I think you two had better come down to the police station," he said. "I want Kien to come, too. We'd better get his story . . . and then get ahold of this boy, Bob."

The police station! Kien's knees buckled under him. Would they put him in jail? Send him back to Vietnam? He turned to Mai. "What can I do?" he whispered. "Little Sister, I—" his words broke off as he saw the expression on Mai's face.

Mai's eyes were full of tears, but she looked angry. "Kien, how could you do this . . . today?" she whispered back fiercely. "Oh, you've ruined my party. You've ruined everything!" Then she turned away from Kien and went into her room.

When Steve and Kien returned from the police station, the house was very quiet. Mai's friends had gone, and all signs of her party had disappeared. Tad and Loc were playing a quiet game in front of the television in the living room, and Diane was in the kitchen. Kien looked around for Mai, but she was nowhere to be seen.

"What happened?" Diane asked, hurrying out of the kitchen.

Steve shrugged. "Once the police reached Kien's friend Bob, there was no problem. The police agreed that Sim attacked Kien and Bob, and that Kien was just defending himself. I was asked if we wanted to press charges against Sim, but I said, no. The boy is in the hospital. He's learned his lesson."

Diane nodded. She gave Kien a funny look. "How is Sim?"

"He almost lost the eye, but he'll be all right." Steve's voice sounded strange, too. "Where's Mai?"

"In her room. The girls were very upset after . . . after what happened, so I took them home."

"I'm sorry," Kien muttered. He wanted to sink down into the floor. Mai had really been looking forward to her party.

Diane went back into the kitchen. After a while, she called, "Hadn't you better get washed up, Kien? We will be having supper soon."

Kien nodded and headed for the bathroom. On the way, he passed Loc and Tad. "I'm glad they didn't throw you in jail," Tad said gravely. Kien nodded and went on without a word. For a second, he hesitated in the hallway, and then he went up to Mai's door and knocked.

"Mai?" he said softly. "I'm back." There was no answer. "I'm sorry about your party," Kien went on. "I really am."

"That's all right." Mai spoke in a determinedly casual voice, and she didn't open the door. "It was a silly party, anyway. I . . . I am glad you aren't in trouble, Kien."

In a way, Kien would have felt better if Mai had

stormed at him. He knew how badly she felt. As he stood awkwardly by the door, he heard her muffled sob, and the sound hurt more than Sim's fists could ever have hurt him.

Eyes misting, he turned to go toward his room, but he was so upset he blundered toward the kitchen. Before he could retreat, he heard Diane say, "I can't get over the fact that he knew just where to hit! He fought to hurt ... to *really* hurt. How did he learn to fight like that?"

"It must have been the survival of the fittest in Vietnam," Steve replied. He spoke forcefully, as if to convince himself. "Kien's gone through things we can't begin to understand."

"I know that, but ... but Mai isn't like that, and Loc isn't that way!" Diane's voice was shaking, she was so upset. "I like Kien, but I can't get through to him. He won't let me get close to him. And now, this."

"What did you want him to do?" Steve demanded. "Did you want Sim Evans to beat him up?"

"Of course not! If Kien had hit or kicked Sim, I'd have understood. It's the *way* he hurt that boy." Diane was silent for a moment, then burst out, "Steve, Sim Evans will come after Kien again. Kien will get known as a troublemaker in school, and he might even get in trouble with the law. How will that affect Mai and Loc?"

Kien heard a slam, as if Steve had smacked his hand against the wall. "Cut it out, Diane! You're making mountains out of molehills. Kien is no troublemaker!"

"Then why did he—?"

"Lower your voice. Do you want the kids to hear?" Steve hissed. "I'll talk to Kien. I'm sure this won't happen again."

Kien backed down the hallway and quietly went into his own room and shut the door. Diane didn't know what to make of him. Steve worried about him. They did not think he was like Mai or Loc ... and they were right. He was not of their blood. Somehow, facing death together had brought them closer than any family could hope to be, and yet ...

I don't belong here to this family, Kien thought. I don't belong anywhere.

Not at school where rules drove him to distraction, not among boys and girls whose thoughts he couldn't always understand, not even to the Olsons, kind as they were, and not to Loc and Mai. "Diane is right," Kien whispered out loud. "I must go away. Sim will come after me when he's well, and it won't be good for Mai and Loc. Even if Sim *doesn't* come after me, they'll be better off if I leave."

With this decision, it was as if something desperate and tense within him quieted and eased. Kien knew now what had to be done. I've been in one place too long, he told himself. I'll leave tonight. He thought of all the places he had been longing to visit—the mountains, the desert, the sea. The sea . . .

Travor! The name leaped into his mind and he jumped in sudden excitement. He recalled the magazine article with the photographs of the happy Vietnamese fisherfolk. He remembered the map Phat Dao had shown him on board the airplane.

"I'll go visit Phat!" Kien exclaimed. "I've got enough money saved. I'll walk to the center of town and take a bus. I will pack now, and after everyone is asleep, I will leave . . . tonight!"

He ran to his dresser and yanked open a drawer, pushing aside socks and underwear to get at his money. As he pulled the cash out, something cool and heavy fell against his hand. With a frown, he pulled it out of the drawer and stood looking at a small bag full of Vietnamese sand.

Instantly, it seemed to Kien that the Olsons' home faded away. He was sitting in a small, fragile boat in the middle of the South China Sea. Mai and Loc slept nearby, exhausted, while across from him sat a bone-thin old man with tender, loving eyes.

"I am dying," Grandfather was saying. "Kien, from this moment you are my oldest grandson. I give you this bag full of precious Vietnamese sand. Take it back to

Vietnam someday. And, my grandson, keep this family together."

Kien shook his head, as if to drive away the memories. "I tried, Grandfather," he whispered. "But don't you see? It can't work. If I stay here, the Olsons will start fighting about me, and Mai and Loc will be unhappy. They are better off without me to ruin their plans and their lives for them."

And yet, the scene moved on in his mind. "You are my oldest grandson," the wise old voice whispered in his ear. "Love has made you so. We do not choose those whom we come to love."

Kien flung the bag of sand away from him. It landed in the wastebasket and fell with a thump. For a second, this thing he had done so horrified Kien that he started forward to retrieve the precious bag. Then he stopped.

"No," he said, "I am right and you're wrong, Grandfather. I have brought Mai and Loc to safety. They are happy here. Now, I have to start thinking of myself. This is *not* my home. Mai and Loc are *not* my family."

Resolutely turning his back on his memories, Kien began to count his money and make his plans.

7

It was dark, an hour before dawn, when Kien left the Olson house. He opened the front door, looking back over his shoulder into the quiet hallway. "Goodby," Kien said softly. "I am going now."

There was only the dark, and silence. The family were all asleep. And, Kien thought, I hope they stay asleep till I am well on my way to Travor.

He closed the door behind him, heard the lock click into place. He waited, listening, but there was no sound. Carrying an airline bag he had packed with clothing, he began to walk toward the road that led to town. It was about an hour's walk to the bus station, and he wanted to be on the first bus to Travor.

Suddenly, he stopped and slapped his thigh with an angry hand. "I'm a fool," he muttered. "I didn't think to bring any food with me!" Last night he had been too upset to eat, and it would probably be some time before he reached Travor. He thought of returning to the Olsons' to get some food, but decided against it. It was too risky. Maybe after I've paid for the bus, I can get myself something to eat, he told himself.

This was an adventure! He began to hum a Vietnamese song as he marched along. He felt as he had felt many years ago when he had moved from village to village in Vietnam. True, he was leaving friends behind, but the world was full of people wanting to be Kien's friends! He began to sing more loudly.

Then, as swiftly as it had begun, Kien's song died away. He remembered when he had last sung that song . . . in the refugee camp at Lam's party. He and Loc and Mai had sung it together.

"That was a different time and place," Kien muttered. He started the song again, defiantly. He didn't care how many memories tried to stop him from going off on his own. He was going!

A sudden blast from an air horn made Kien jump. A large truck had pulled up a little behind him, and the truck driver was leaning out of the window. "Hey, buddy!" the driver called. "Want a ride downtown?"

Kien nodded eagerly and ran to the truck. It was a ten-wheeler, and when Kien hopped in beside the driver, he felt as if he were high in the air, overlooking the world. "Thank you," he said, with his best grin. "I going bus."

"Bus station, eh?" The truck driver gave Kien a curious look. "Why are you heading for the bus so early in the day? Running away from home?"

Kien laughed as if this was a very good joke. "Oh, no! Oh, no! I go see family. They live far away."

"Whereabouts do they live?"

"Far away," Kien repeated vaguely. If Steve ever decided to trace Kien, he might track down this truck driver and talk to him. "Far away" could mean just about anywhere!

The truck driver set his rig in motion. "Where do you come from, son?" he asked. "You Japanese? Korean?"

"I Vietnamese."

The man raised his eyebrows. "I'll be. You must be one of those boat people that are coming over here all the time."

Kien felt somewhat uncomfortable. This man seemed friendly, but he was big and reminded Kien a little of

Sim Evans' father. He thought of some way to change the subject.

"This is fine truck," he said admiringly. "I like very much!"

The driver began to tell Kien about the truck and how he had saved for many years to buy it. "It cost mucho money, but it was worth it," he said, patting the steering wheel lovingly with a big hand. "Remember this, boy. In this country, if you work hard enough, you can get ahead. You can make something of yourself."

Kien nodded, his eyes on the sky. The dawn was turning the horizon a soft pinkish-gray. He wondered if anyone was up at the Olsons'. They would not notice that he was gone, of course . . . not until Diane or Steve came to wake him to go to school.

"No place like America," the truck driver was saying. "No, sir. No place like home!"

Kien listened to the driver talk and nodded or shook his head, all the while planning what to do when he got to Travor. They would surely welcome him there, and he would greet them so gladly. It would be good not to have to talk this strange, slippery English all the time. He would stay with Phat Dao for a while, and then move on and see more of the country.

"Here we are, son," the truck driver said. He slowed as he approached the bus depot. "Good luck on your travels, now. Hope you get to your folks okay."

Kien thanked him and got out with his bag bouncing at his heels. He started to walk toward the terminal, then stopped short as the truck driver suddenly shouted, "Hey . . . wait!"

What had gone wrong? Kien's heart began to pound. Perhaps the truck driver had become suspicious about something. What should I do? Kien wondered. Perhaps I'd better run away as fast as I can!

"Come back here, boy!" the truck driver yelled.

Kien turned slowly and made himself face the man.

"C'mere," the driver called, and when Kien came nearer, thrust a few dollars into his hand. "You take this and buy yourself some breakfast. My kid's your age, and he's always hungry . . . and broke!"

Kien was too astonished to thank him. The driver waved, and was gone. Kien waved till the big rig was out of sight and then turned back to the bus depot, feeling ready to start singing all over again. An adventure, he told himself. A real adventure is beginning!

Inside the bus depot, he bought a ticket to Travor. Now Kien was grateful for the truck driver's money. The ticket cost much more than he had planned! When he had counted out all the change he had left, he had only a dollar.

"I'll wait till I get to Travor to eat," Kien said to himself, ignoring his growling stomach. The man who had sold him the ticket had said the ride would take a few hours. "Only a few hours," Kien consoled himself. "Then I can eat good Vietnamese food again."

He sat down on the long, wooden depot bench to wait and dream of Vietnamese food. Good, spicy food; not the tasteless, boring Western fare. He was thinking of a bowl of delicious noodles when the bus roared into the depot. The clock on the wall said six thirty. Kien hopped on board, found himself a seat near the back. "Soon," he whispered, "I'll be in Travor!"

But "soon" turned out to be much later. Shortly after leaving the bus depot, the bus broke down. They did not get under way again for over an hour, and then, at noon, the driver stopped at a depot beside a large restaurant.

"Lunchtime, folks!" the bus driver announced. "Stretch those legs and fill your stomachs. We'll lay over for forty minutes."

Kien wished that the driver hadn't mentioned food. His stomach had begun to complain loudly. Following the other passengers into the restaurant, Kien watched hungrily as people picked up trays and moved through the cafeteria-style food line. He bought himself a small carton of milk—all he could afford. "I need to keep *some* money on hand for when I get to Travor," Kien reasoned.

The milk cost thirty cents. Kien took it to a booth in back of the restaurant, where he need not see other people eating, and sipped the milk through a straw. As he was sipping, a woman with two small boys in tow came to sit nearby. The little boys had big hamburgers and french fries piled onto their plates, and the smells of meat and potatoes drifted into Kien's hungry nose. He wished they would hurry and eat their food, but no, the little boys were not hungry, and their mother started scolding them for wasting the good meat.

"There are starving people in this world," she told her sons. "If you don't eat your nice hamburgers, you won't get any ice cream!"

Ice cream! Kien's mouth watered as he thought of cool, sweet, rich ice cream. He desperately wanted an ice cream, but he knew he couldn't afford it.

Everyone around Kien was eating. They were eating and eating! Pies, milk shakes, steaks, mounds of french fries, sandwiches, sodas . . . Kien had never seen so much food! I have to get out of here before I feel sick, he thought. Swallowing the last of his milk, he got up, just as the woman rose, also.

She was very annoyed. "If you won't eat, you won't, but remember—no ice cream! And this is the last time I bring you to a restaurant!" She piled uneaten food on her tray, and Kien saw the boys' untouched hamburgers join the rest of the food.

"If only I could grab one of those hamburgers," Kien muttered yearningly. He watched as the woman passed, the tray of half-eaten and uneaten food in her hands. He groaned out loud as the food was thrown into a big trash can nearby.

"Don't be slobs," the woman told her sons. "Throw your napkins in here, boys."

Kien followed the little boys as they dropped their napkins into the trash can. He threw his own empty milk carton into the trash, along with big chunks of steak, vegetables, untouched rolls.

"All those days we were without food," he muttered,

remembering the long, windswept days on the South China Sea when he and Mai and Loc had divided a banana into four pieces, with Mai offering her share to the sick old Grandfather. There was anger in him as he turned and almost ran out of the restaurant. "People are starving," the woman had said, yet she threw good food away!

I do not understand America, Kien said to himself. And yet, and yet, there were good people here, too. He thought of the truck driver who had pushed money into his hands.

Finally the passengers got back into the bus, and the journey to Travor resumed. It was late afternoon, however, before they reached Kien's destination. He got out of the bus, stretched all over, and rested his bag on the ground as he took a good look around. From the bus depot, Kien could see a long stretch of road flanked by many shops and buildings. Travor looked like just another town . . . except that it was shabbier than most.

Kien picked up his bag and began to walk. The dusty gold sunlight softened the sharp outlines of buildings along the main street, but Travor didn't look like the photos Kien had seen in the magazine. Where was the sea? Kien asked himself. And, more important, where were the Vietnamese? His stomach gave a great growl and asked a question of its own. Where was food?

"There goes one of them!"

Surprised, Kien turned around. An American boy was lounging against a telephone pole, watching him. Had the boy been talking to him? Kien smiled and waved a hand in greeting, but the boy ignored this friendly gesture and turned his back.

"Oh, well," Kien murmured. He hadn't come to Travor to make friends with anyone. The important thing was to find where the Vietnamese people were living. He started to walk again, and then saw something up ahead that made him smile. There stood a small diner with a blinking neon sign. He would order something cheap—milk again, maybe—and ask for directions.

The diner was almost empty. As Kien came in, a few people who were sitting around the counter on stools turned to look at him. A large, dark-haired man sitting in a booth near the door half rose, then sank back into his seat. Kien turned to the waitress behind the counter.

"Please excuse. . . ," he began.

The waitress ignored him and walked to the opposite end of the counter, where she proceeded to wipe the counter top with a cloth. Perhaps she didn't hear me, Kien reasoned. He eased himself up onto a stool by the counter and stared hungrily at the menu that was printed on the wall. Sandwiches, he read, seventy cents. Well, he had enough money for a sandwich!

The waitress walked by Kien again, but made no sign that she had seen him. Kien cleared his throat. "Excuse. . . ," he began again.

Now she turned to face him, her face blank. "I'm sorry," she said. "We're closed."

Kien blinked. Closed? But people were eating and drinking all around him! Had he mistaken her meaning? "Excuse please, I want sandwich," he said.

"Don't you understand English? We're closed!" the waitress snapped. Her eyes were unfriendly. "You have to go."

Kien's insides gave a desperate gurgle. Then the big, black-haired man in the booth spoke up. "Margie, is he giving you any trouble?"

"No trouble. He's leaving, Paul." The waitress turned her back on Kien.

Kien couldn't understand any of this. He looked at the dark-haired man, trying to explain what he wanted, that he needed directions, but stopped when he saw the look in the man's deep-set gray eyes. They were Sim Evans' eyes in another face. This man hated Kien!

"Get out of here," the big man rumbled.

Kien got up so quickly he nearly tripped over his bag. He snatched up the bag and hurried outside. As the door banged behind him he heard the waitress say,

"Honestly! The nerve! Why can't they stay where they belong?"

Kien was more puzzled than angry. He began to walk away from the diner, then stopped. He still hadn't found out where the Vietnamese people lived. He looked about to see if there was some way of getting this information and then spotted a policeman directing traffic at an intersection a block or so away. The policeman would know.

Kien hurried up to the officer. "Please excuse. . . ," he began politely.

The policeman gave him a harassed look. "What do you want?" he demanded.

"I lost." Kien tried a friendly smile, but the policeman didn't smile back. "I need to know where Vietnamese live."

"Another one," the officer muttered. In a louder voice he added, "Okay. Go straight down this road, then turn left." Kien nodded. "Go three more blocks, and you'll come to a set of traffic lights. Walk a mile or so beyond the lights, and then turn on Bullard Road. This will take you to Wilshire Street. That's where the Vietnamese rent their houses."

"Wilshire Street," Kien repeated. "Thank you, sir." The policeman nodded curtly, and Kien walked away, muttering the directions under his breath. They were confusing, but he thought he had them right. Left, then right . . . or was it right, then go left? He half turned to ask the policeman to repeat his directions, then saw that the black-haired man from the restaurant had walked across the street and was speaking to the police officer. Both men were nodding and staring after Kien.

Kien hurried on his way feeling uneasy and unhappy. The great adventure did not seem so exciting anymore. What was wrong with these people, anyway? The magazine article had told of happy, friendly people in Travor. Well, where were they? Kien had a sudden, horrible thought. Could he have come to the *wrong* Travor?

A stray wind caught at Kien's shirt. The sun was be-

ginning to set and it would soon be dark. He needed to
find Wilshire Street as soon as he could. Kien began to
quicken his step, then saw something that made him
stop. A telephone booth stood by the side of the street.

"I left without a word or explanation," Kien muttered.
"I should telephone them and tell them that I'm safe."

He pulled out his remaining seventy cents, looked at
the coins, then went over to the booth. He dropped a
dime into the coin slot and gave the operator the Olsons'
number. "I wish to call collect," he said, repeating the
words Steve had taught him to use in an emergency.
Then he waited as the phone rang once, twice.

Then Mai's voice said, "Hello?"

Instantly he remembered the warmth of the kitchen—
fragrant with Diane's chocolate-chip brownies—Steve Olson's laugh, the sound of two little boys playing in the
backyard, and Mai's face.

"Will you accept a collect call from Kien Ho?" the operator was asking.

"Kien? Oh, Kien! Yes, I will accept!" Mai shouted. She
sounded beside herself. "Kien, where are you?"

"I'm fine, Mai. I called to tell you that I'm all right,"
Kien began, in Vietnamese.

Mai's voice cracked. "Kien, what happened? I saw the
bag of sand and I knew. . . . Why did you run away
from us?"

"Listen"—Kien wet his dry lips—"Mai, it's best this
way. I am not a part of your family. I am only your
adopted brother. You and Loc fit in so well with the Olsons' life and I don't. I just have to find out where I belong, that's all."

Mai was crying. "You belong with us! Oh, Kien,
please, *please* come back home. We are lost without
you. Diane has been crying all day, and she and Steve
are going crazy with worry and . . . Kien you *are* our
big brother. Grandfather said—"

Kien hung up. The phone receiver made a clicking
sound, and it seemed as if something, a tie between the
past and the present, had snapped. Kien drew a deep

breath as he stepped out of the booth. "It's for the best," he whispered to himself.

"There he goes! There!"

Kien swung around. Three high school age boys stood behind him. One of them he recognized as the boy he had seen earlier near the bus depot. This boy now held a baseball bat and was tapping it against his thigh.

"Run him out of town!" another boy spat out. "What does he think he is?"

Me? Kien wondered. He stared as the three moved toward him. Yes, they did mean him!

He started to run, his bag bouncing at his side. Behind him, the three youths ran, too. "Don't let him get away!" yelled the one with the baseball bat. "We'll teach him a lesson this time!"

A rock whizzed past Kien's ear, another hit him in the shoulder. Dull pain radiated through his arm. "What'll I do?" Kien gasped. He couldn't keep running like this. Already, the breath was bursting in his lungs. He would have to stop, face these boys. And then what?

"Boy, over here! Quick!"

Kien now heard another sound, a roaring noise. A motorcycle had pulled up alongside him, and the rider was motioning to him with a gloved hand. "Behind me!" the motorcycle rider shouted. "Jump!"

Kien lunged. He landed astraddle behind this stranger. He clung to him as the man gunned his engine to full power.

A howl of angry protest filled the air behind Kien. The motorcycle thundered away down the street, and Kien glanced quickly over his shoulder. For a split second, he saw the angry, hate-filled faces of the three who had pursued him. One of them shook a fist.

"We'll get you yet!" he yelled.

Kien shivered. The boy meant what he said. The question was . . . *Why?*

8

Kien watched the three disappear into a haze of dust. He shivered.

"If they'd caught you, they would have torn you apart," his rescuer said. "Their fathers probably work for Paul."

"Paul?" Kien remembered the big, dark-haired man with the hating eyes.

"Paul Orrin. Everyone knows Paul Orrin!"

"I just now come Travor, look for relatives. My name Kien. Not knowing Paul Orrin."

The rider stopped the motorcycle, turned to look Kien over. Kien looked back, interested. His rescuer was not a very tall man, but he had powerful shoulders and a broad chest to match. His mustache and beard and curly reddish hair made him look like one of the Vikings that Mr. Hunter had told Kien about back in Bradley.

"I'm Bill Ransom," he said, holding out a broad, strong-looking hand. "Glad to know you, Kien."

"I glad too. Thank you for what you do, Mr. Ransom."

"Call me Bill." Kien liked Bill's wide, friendly smile and the steady look in his gray eyes. "Where do your relatives live? I'll take you there."

Kien remembered the street the policeman had

named. "Wilshire Street," he said. Bill nodded and started the motorcycle again.

"Why three boys want hurt me?" Kien shouted over the roar of the cycle. "Why Paul Orrin not liking me?"

"It's not you, personally. Travor is about the worst place for a Vietnamese right now," Bill shouted back.

That wasn't possible! Kien frowned. That photograph of Travor he had seen. "Vietnamese not fishermen here?" he asked.

"There are Vietnamese fishermen here. That's the problem. Paul Orrin doesn't like the Vietnamese fishermen."

"But why? They are doing bad things?"

Bill was silent for a moment, then slowed his cycle so he need not shout to be heard. "In the beginning, when the Vietnamese first came here to Travor, nobody minded, not even Orrin or the fishermen who work for him. There were plenty of fish in the sea."

"Fish go away?" Kien was trying to puzzle this out.

"The fish are still there. Plenty of fish. Rock crabs and rockfish, white sea bass, mackerel and bonito, even salmon sometimes. This is what happened, Kien. The first few Vietnamese fishermen came here, found life good in Travor. They brought over their friends and relatives. Then, someone wrote an article about Travor and it was published in a magazine. Soon more and more Vietnamese were coming to this town. They bought a fishing boat, then another, then several more. They leased three run-down houses out on the pier, and settled down to fish and live. They worked very hard and sold their catch more cheaply than did the American fishermen."

Kien began to understand. Sim Evans' father had lost his job to a Vietnamese who took less pay than he did.

"The American fishermen started to get nervous," Bill continued. "They were afraid that the Vietnamese would take away their means of making a living. Then, Paul Orrin stepped in."

Bill guided his motorcycle down a dark street. The

buildings here were mostly warehouses, with lightless windows that stared down like blind eyes. Kien did not like this place. Surely this couldn't be where the Vietnamese lived? Yet, when he breathed deeply, he smelled the familiar tang of the sea.

"Paul Orrin, Kien, is one of the most important people in Travor," Bill explained. "He has a lot of money, and he has built up a fishing corporation. Most of the fishermen in Travor either owe Paul money on boats he has sold them, or they work for him. He owns other property, too—restaurants, apartments. So when he speaks, people listen."

"I understand." Kien remembered how the policeman and Paul Orrin had been nodding together. "What Orrin say?"

"He said that the Vietnamese were troublemakers and should be forced to leave Travor," Bill said bluntly. "He said that if the Vietnamese stay, fishermen in Travor will be ruined. He's asked for a special town meeting about this, and he's asked a special committee to study what he calls the 'Vietnamese Problem.'"

They had reached the Vietnamese community. Three houses, in not much better repair than the vacant warehouses they had passed, stood by the side of the road. Bill pulled his motorcycle up to the sidewalk in front of the largest of the three houses.

"Huy Dao lives here, with his wife and daughter and his nephew Phat," he told Kien. "Huy Dao's the leader of the Vietnamese community. He'll direct you to your relatives."

Kien got off the cycle. "Thanks, Bill." He paused, then asked, "You not hating Vietnamese?"

Bill's teeth shone white in a grin. "I'm too busy to hate anyone, Kien. I run a Marina store—the only one in Travor—where fishermen get their supplies. I have Vietnamese customers, and I find they're not any different from my American customers. I also have a good friend, Phat Dao." He started to gun his engine, then stopped. "Remind Phat about the special town meeting, will you,

Kien? It's to be held tomorrow night, at the high school. It's very important that all the Vietnamese are at that meeting."

Kien nodded and waved as Bill roared away on his motorcycle. It was a stroke of luck that Bill had brought him right to Phat Dao's house, but he suddenly felt exhausted, and his head ached. He wanted to sit down on the pavement and put his head in his hands, but just then a breeze carried delicious food smells right to his nose.

Kien's fatigue disappeared. His stomach gave a mighty gurgle as he hurried up the front steps of the house. The steps were rotting away, and Kien had to walk carefully. What a place to live! Kien thought, as he knocked on the door.

"Who is there?" a woman's suspicious voice demanded.

Kien automatically assumed a humble, pleading tone, the voice of a street beggar. "Kind Aunt, this is Kien, a stranger, looking for shelter."

The heavy wooden door cracked open a little, and a tall, gaunt woman stuck her face through the crack. Narrow dark eyes looked Kien over. "Are you alone, boy? Where are your parents?"

"I have no father, no mother." The whine in Kien's voice grew stronger. "I have been terrified and beaten in this town. A man called Bill Ransom saved me from the townspeople and brought me here."

"Phat's friend," the woman murmured. She hesitated, then commanded, "Wait." With that, she shut the door in Kien's face.

Kien waited, counting the long moments. The food smells made his mouth water. He was just about to knock on the door again when it opened, and a small man, perhaps an inch taller than Kien, stood in the doorway.

"I am Huy Dao," the man said in a deep bass voice. "The people here call me *Bác* Huy . . . Uncle Huy." He looked Kien over critically, and Kien noted that though

Bác Huy was small, he had powerful arms and shoulders. I wouldn't want to wrestle with him, Kien thought.

"You say you are an orphan?" Bác Huy had large, somewhat fierce dark eyes. Kien shifted a little uneasily as the man went on, "How did you get to this country?"

Kien thought up several lies, then decided he had better tell this little man as much of the truth as he could. "I came over to live with a sponsor, Bác Huy, but I didn't like it where I lived. A boy at the school I went to beat me and called me names. I didn't feel I belonged, so I ran away. I am now looking for a place to stay."

Bác Huy said nothing, but he pulled the door wider and nodded to Kien to come in. "You can stay with us for a while, anyway," he said. "Thuyet, give this boy something to eat."

The gaunt woman scowled. "Am I to feed every beggar's brat that walks in off the street?" she shrilled. "I have enough to do, getting ready for your meeting tonight!"

"I'll help, Mother." Kien hadn't noticed the girl who was standing in the dark hallway close to the door. She was a few years younger than Kien and had a cheerful round face framed by two short braids.

"Very well, Linh." Bác Huy's eyes became less fierce as he smiled at the girl, and even Thuyet seemed to soften. Still she kept on grumbling.

"There's hardly enough food for the rest of us," she snorted. "This brat will eat everything we have in the house."

Thuyet led the way through the hall and into a large room where a big table was surrounded by ramshackle chairs. The room had been scrubbed clean, but there were huge water stains on the ceiling, and there was a smell of mildew. Beyond this room was a small, dark kitchen from which issued delicious smells. Kien's stomach gave an enormous rumble.

Thuyet sniffed. She pointed to a corner of the kitchen where stood a rickety table and a few chairs. Linh patted a chair with a smile. "Sit here," she invited. "This is where my cousin Phat sits when he is home. He's a hard worker, my cousin. All day he works on the *Seagull* with my father, and at night he washes dishes in the town. That is where he is now."

Kien hardly heard what Linh was saying. His entire concentration was on the dish of noodles Thuyet put before him. Kien seized chopsticks and began to eat. The good food filled his cheeks and throat, and he could feel the nourishment trickling down into his stomach. The bowl emptied almost at once.

Thuyet clicked her tongue. "Are you eating for the whole world?" But she filled the bowl again, and again Kien wolfed the bowlful down and even licked the bowl. As he ate, someone knocked on the outer door.

"Perhaps Phat has returned," Thuyet said to Linh, who hurried out of the kitchen to see.

Now that the worst of his hunger pangs were appeased, Kien tried to think up some way of softening the hard-eyed Thuyet's heart. "I met your nephew Phat Dao on the airplane coming to this country," he told Thuyet. "The world is a small place, Kind Aunt."

"Maybe." Thuyet pointed a skinny finger at Kien. "Small or not, however, you aren't getting another bite of food out of me! And never mind this 'Kind Aunt.'"

Kien sighed. Usually women wanted to feed him and take care of him. Thuyet apparently wanted to do neither. She glared at him, folding her arms across her chest. How different Thuyet was from Diane Olson, for instance, who always baked those special brownies for him.

Kien got up quickly, pushing the thought from his mind. "I thank you for the fine food," he said. "If I can do anything—"

"I doubt it." Thuyet sniffed loudly. "Go into the other room and listen to what Bác Huy has to say at the meeting. And keep out of my kitchen! *Cam vao!*"

Kien left the kitchen and reentered the large room. By now, several men were sitting around the table, and others stood in clumps, all quietly talking. All in all, Kien counted thirty-three men in the room. Some of them looked at Kien curiously, so Bác Huy explained.

"This boy is Kien. He has come here to stay with us for a while."

Kien sat down in a corner of the room and made himself comfortable. He was wondering what this meeting was all about, when Bác Huy said, "It is late. We had better start this meeting without waiting for Phat to return from town."

The men settled down at once, some sitting around the table, others standing or sitting on the floor. Bác Huy cleared his throat. "Brothers, we are meeting tonight because we must discuss our trouble here in Travor. Trinh, you said that there were angry words today when you weighed your catch at the pier and tried to sell to the dealers."

A man as thin as a length of straw nodded. "It is so, Bác Huy. Three American fishermen who work for Paul Orrin did not want me to weigh my fish or sell it. They tried to throw my catch back into the sea. I tell you, I'm getting sick of Travor."

A loud murmur ran around the table. "This can't go on," another man spoke up. "Women at the supermarket said insulting things to my wife yesterday. What kind of life is this?"

Bác Huy pounded a fist on the table, as everyone began to talk at once. "We've come to discuss this, not to shout at the same time!" he bellowed. "Trinh, I know how you feel." He lifted a heavy fist and shook it in the air. "I would like to hit that Paul Orrin! But my nephew—"

"Your nephew begs you to be calm, Uncle," a new voice said. Kien looked toward the door and saw that a young man had come in. It was Phat from the plane, but a sunburned, tired-looking Phat. "We can't solve anything by fighting these people," Phat continued. "And remember, not everyone in Travor hates us."

"Paul Orrin hates us!" Trinh retorted.

Bác Huy pounded on the table again, and Thuyet

came out of the kitchen to snap, "You are like a bunch of water buffalo, with your noise!"

"Paul Orrin hates us, because he thinks we are going to ruin his fishing business," Phat argued. "For many years, Paul Orrin has made money in Travor. He owns property and many fishing boats. Most people in town owe him money, or are afraid of him because they work for him, so they do not speak out against him. But not everyone feels the way Orrin does! Bill Ransom of the Marina store, for instance."

Kien pricked up his ears, but Trinh snorted, "Bill Ransom. He may be your friend, Phat, but is he our friend?"

"He trades with us fairly at his Marina, and he gives us credit," Bác Huy said slowly. "But perhaps that is because he is a businessman and wants to make money."

Phat looked angry. "That's not true! Bill is my friend, and he's your friend, too. He helped me get my job at the restaurant."

"Washing dishes!" Thuyet snorted. "A fine job for a man who wants to be a lawyer."

"Aunt, Bill will help me get back to school so I *can* be a lawyer someday. I say he is our friend!"

Kien couldn't keep quiet any longer. He bounced up, saying, "It's true!" As all eyes, including Phat's, turned to him, he added, "Bill saved me from a beating tonight."

Phat looked very astonished. "I remember you from the plane. Your name is Kien, isn't it?" Kien nodded. "How . . . when did you get here?"

So Kien told them the story of his leaving his sponsor's home, and about the youths who had attacked him in Travor. He embroidered on the adventure to make a more interesting story, and was pleased to see that even Thuyet listened spellbound. When the story was over, Phat nodded, looking pleased.

"I told you Bill Ransom was a friend! And he will be our friend tomorrow at the special town meeting."

Kien now remembered Bill's message to Phat. The Vietnamese, who had been silently listening, now began to mutter among themselves.

"Bác Huy," Trinh said, "what do you think of this meeting? Should we go at all?"

Bác Huy frowned thoughtfully. "I don't know. Somehow, I think it will be a waste of time. Talking never solved anything."

"But we must go!" Phat urged. "It's our chance to be heard by this town."

Kien had been listening with growing excitement. This was getting interesting!

"I will go to the town meeting with you, Phat!" he cried. Then, as everyone turned to look at him, he added with a grin, "I want to hear what this Special Committee of Orrin's has to say."

"What lies, you mean!" Bác Huy retorted, but he nodded slowly. "Even so, we will go. We will take our families along with us. Thus we will show Orrin that we speak as a group."

"It's the only way to get fair treatment," Phat said earnestly. "We've got to speak up for ourselves."

Bác Huy grunted without much conviction. "That's all very well," he said. "But will Orrin want to listen?"

9

Bác Huy's house was home to Phat and two other families besides. All the rooms in the house were taken, so Kien slept on the floor in the big room, on a very thin mat. He was so tired he slept well, without dreams, but when he woke he looked around him, wondering where he could be. Then he heard Thuyet's scolding voice in the kitchen and remembered that he was in Travor.

What an adventure this is, he said to himself. I wonder what will happen today.

It was not quite five by Kien's watch, but the household was awake and full of life. Kien could hear the sound of feet tramping around as he folded his uncomfortable little sleeping mat.

"Ah, you're up, Kien." Bác Huy came striding into the big room. "Fishermen have to get up early. Did we waken you?"

Suddenly, Kien had the urge to feel the deck of a fishing boat under his feet again. "Could I come fishing with you, Bác Huy?" he asked.

The little man frowned, then smiled. "Why not? But I warn you, it'll be hard work. You'd better have something to eat first."

Phat and Trinh and another man were already in the dark little kitchen eating rice and drinking tea. Thuyet

muttered something under her breath when she saw
Kien, but Phat smiled a welcome and shifted over so
that the boy could sit next to him. "Are you coming to
sea with us?" Phat asked. "Perhaps you should stay on
land today and save your strength for the meeting
tonight."

"Do you think there will be trouble?" Kien asked, his
mouth full. Trinh gave Kien a disgusted look.

"Can fish swim?" he demanded. "Bác Huy, I don't
think it's such a good idea to go to this meeting. The
Americans have already decided we're to blame for
everything."

"It would be best to eat our breakfast and start our
work for the day," Bác Huy said. "We'll think about the
meeting later. Right now, we have to think of fish!"

The little leader took one last gulp of tea and got up.
The others did the same, and Kien followed them out of
the house. The morning chill goosepimpled Kien's arms,
and Phat slid a windbreaker off his shoulders. "Here," he
told Kien. "Wear this. It can get cool out at sea."

Together, they walked toward the pier. In the
darkness now faintly lined with gray, Kien saw several
boats returning from a night's fishing. Other fishing craft
were moored close together, most of them outboard-
powered skiffs. Next to the skiffs Kien noticed some
larger, powerful fishing craft. Orrin's? he wondered.

"This way," Phat called.

Many fishermen, both American and Vietnamese, were
busy with their boats. Kien followed Phat and Bác Huy
to a boat nearby. "This one is the *Seagull*," Bác Huy
said. "Isn't she beautiful? We bought this one soon after
we came to Travor."

Kien nodded wordlessly, remembering a Vietnamese
fishing boat crafted with love by a man in a village
thousands of miles away. The *Sea Breeze* had carried his
family to safety. Only . . .

Only, Mai and Loc are not my family anymore, Kien
reminded himself.

"We bought the *Seagull* with the money we made

catching and selling fish," Bác Huy said. His voice was suddenly passionate. "We will not be chased away from this place. If necessary, we will fight to stay here!"

"We're ready to get under way, Uncle." Kien saw a worried look in Phat's eyes. As Bác Huy got into the *Seagull*, Kien sat next to the young man.

"Do you think it'll come to fighting?" he whispered.

Phat did not answer as the *Seagull* pulled rapidly away from the land. Then he said, "Uncle is a man of action, not words. He would have fought Paul Orrin with his fists if I hadn't stopped him." He shook his head. "Nothing can be gained by violence, and anyway, how do we fight a whole town?"

"Is talking better?"

"There are good people here. It would be a fine place to live, if we can work this out peacefully."

Phat would have gone on, except that Bác Huy bawled at them, saying that it was time to fish, not gossip like old women around cooking pots.

There was plenty to do. Kien remembered muscles he hadn't used in months. The sky was turning dove gray when they finally reached a point where the net was lowered into the water. Phat instructed Kien, saying, "I am learning more and more about fishing. At first, it was hard. I was never trained to be a fisherman. But I have come to respect the fish."

Kien couldn't help laughing. "How do you respect a fish?"

"Well, fish can be brave and resourceful. Take the salmon, for instance. It is spawned in a freshwater river miles away from the sea, but when it is grown strong enough, instincts urge it to find a way downstream to the ocean. The salmon lives most of its life in the sea, but at a certain time of life it has another urge . . . to return to the freshwater river of its beginnings. Back goes the salmon, across miles and miles of sea, up rivers and sometimes even waterfalls! Some die on the way, others succeed in finding their home." Phat was silent for a moment, then added softly, "They know what they want and are willing to die to find their homes again."

Kien felt a prickling down his spine. Phat wasn't talking just about fish.

"To me, Travor is home," Phat added.

The sun was rising steadily, blood red in a haze of early summer cloud. "It's going to be hot today," Bác Huy announced. "Perhaps a storm will cool things off. We could use some rain around here. It's been too dry lately."

But this dryness did not affect the fish. Kien helped haul quantities of unwary fish into the boat. Most of the catch, Phat explained, would be weighed and sold to men who came right down to the docks to do their trading. These were owners of large restaurants, wholesalers, men who wanted fish in bulk. On a good day, a lot of fish would pass hands.

For the next few hours, they toiled away. Kien's back ached by the time the *Seagull* returned to the pier with a full load of silvery fish. Here, women and those children not in school helped unload the catch, which was then weighed and sold to waiting customers. Kien noted that while this was going on, many American fishermen stood around and glared at the Vietnamese. Kien heard muttered remarks, and one of the men spat close to Bác Huy's foot.

"Lousy foreigners, taking away our business," the man snarled. "Just wait till tonight. You'll get yours!"

There were mutters of agreement from the other American fishermen. The Vietnamese took no notice, but Kien could see that Bác Huy's fierce face was turning redder and redder with suppressed anger. Kien knew that it cost Bác Huy a lot to stay silent, but quiet he remained until the last of the *Seagull's* catch had been weighed and sold. Then the Vietnamese turned to go . . . and almost ran right into a big, broad-shouldered man with dark hair.

Bác Huy's face turned purple. Kien was sure he was

going to burst. "Get out of way, Paul Orrin!" Bác Huy spat in English.

"You get out of mine, Huy Dao!" Orrin snarled right back. Kien saw the little man's muscles tighten and his hands go into fists. Phat grabbed his uncle by the shoulder and hustled him out of Paul Orrin's way.

"That is not the way to do things!" Phat whispered furiously. "They *want* you to start a fight, my Uncle, don't you see? Then they can claim that the Vietnamese are troublemakers."

Kien glanced over his shoulder at Paul Orrin, who was standing with his fingers hooked into his belt, watching the Vietnamese leave. Behind Orrin, the American fishermen of Travor had formed a solid line. Their faces were anything but friendly.

No need to make trouble, Kien thought. It's already here!

When the work of the day was done, the men returned to Bác Huys' house to rest, bathe, and prepare for the meeting. The kitchen was crowded with tired fishermen, so Kien took his rice bowl and went to sit on the outside step. From where he sat he could see the ocean.

Kien tried to imagine what it would be like to be a salmon, braving the wide sea in search of home. What an adventure that would be! The fish had no guarantee that it would ever reach home, but at least it knew it *had* a home.

"If you don't eat your rice, it will get cold," Linh said. She had come out of the house and now sat down on the step beside Kien. She had on a pink dress and there were pink ribbons tied at the ends of her braids.

"Do you like my dress?" she asked Kien.

"It's all right."

"It's my best dress, for school. I used to love going to school here until the trouble came. Now I hate it. The other children say bad things to me, and one girl slapped and punched me because she said her father had to sell their home and move away from Travor. She said it was the fault of us Vietnamese."

Kien chewed his rice thoughtfully. "What did Bác Huy do?"

"He was very angry. He wanted to take me out of school. Phat told him to do nothing, though, because it would only make things worse." Linh sighed. "Do you think tonight's meeting will make things better for us?"

The door of the house swung open. Bác Huy came out, followed by Phat, Thuyet, and the others. "It is almost time to go," he said to Kien. "Are you ready?"

It was early. Because the Vietnamese did not own cars, they were going to walk to Travor High School. The high school was three miles away, and because of the children that were to come with the group, they would have to go slowly. As Bác Huy explained this to Kien, men, women, and children from the Vietnamese community came out of the houses and gathered around their little leader.

"Tell us again what to do at the meeting," someone suggested, and Bác Huy nodded at Phat to speak.

"This is what will happen," Phat explained. "The Special Committee will tell the townspeople what it has found out. The Committee will suggest ways to solve the problem. Then, the town will vote by crying out 'Yea' or 'Nay'. We are townspeople also, so we will have a chance to vote. If the Committee's suggestions are not good ones, we will be able to vote against them."

"I wonder," Kien heard Bác Huy mutter, but he said nothing out loud and, family by family, the community began to walk. Kien walked with Linh and Thuyet, behind Bác Huy and Phat. Nobody said very much, and nobody looked too happy.

As they walked along the long row of deserted warehouses and onto a road leading to the center of town, a car passed them. A woman leaned out of the car to shout, "Hey, Vietnamese! Go home!"

Kien felt a rush of anger. Did that woman know what she was saying? Did she know about Vietnam, and how refugees by the thousand had taken to the sea because they *had* no home?

As they walked on, more and more cars passed the Vietnamese. Most of these cars drove by in silence, but others were full of passengers who shouted insults at the walkers. We don't seem to have many friends here, Kien thought.

But he was wrong. As they passed through the center of town, Kien's eye caught a large sign above a store. The sign read "RANSOM'S MARINA," and Bill Ransom was standing in front of the store, waiting. When he saw Phat, Bill walked over to greet his friend.

"I decided to walk along with you," he said. "Just in case."

Phat said nothing, but the two men shook hands. Bác Huy frowned. "Nephew, tell this one that it is not necessary for him to walk with us Vietnamese," he snapped.

Phat put his hand on Bác Huy's arm. "Uncle, Bill is our friend. He walks with us so that there may be no trouble. We should welcome him."

Nothing more was said. They walked on, passing various shops, houses, and stores. Many other men and women, too, came to join Bill Ransom and the Vietnamese. When Kien finally sighted the large, flat-topped high school, about fifteen Americans were walking with the Vietnamese community.

But these friends were few compared to the townspeople who waited in the high school parking lot, or who thronged the steps. Linh put her hand in Kien's as they turned into the walkway that led to the school building.

"They don't look friendly," Linh whispered. Kien didn't blame her for sounding scared.

What am I doing here? he asked himself. This has nothing to do with me! Last night, coming to the meeting had sounded like a grand adventure. But now . . .

Kien nearly turned right around and ran away when he saw a knot of men standing in the walkway, blocking their path. These men had weather-browned faces and were carrying signs that read: "Vietnamese, go! Travor doesn't want you!"

"Orrin's people," Bill said to Phat, who nodded.

"Pay no attention," he warned Bác Huy and the others. "They will let us pass if we say and do nothing."

The sign wielders stepped aside for the Vietnamese, but they waved their signs in Phat's face. One of them called, "Why're you walking with these Vietnamese, Bill Ransom? Aren't Americans good enough for you anymore?"

A low, angry growl came from the other men and another shouted, "Supposing we just take our trade somewhere else, Bill?"

Bill stopped short and faced this man. "We've done business for five years, Jeb Little," he said in a strong voice. "I've given you more credit than was good for my business, too. If you want to do business someplace else, go right ahead! That goes for you, Sam Reubin, and you, Ed McKenny!"

Muttering, but sounding somewhat ashamed, the sign bearers dropped back and let the Vietnamese climb the front steps of the school. Kien followed as Bill led them through heavy swinging doors into a hallway thronged with more people.

"Here's the school auditorium," Bill said. "This is where the meeting will be held."

The auditorium was much like the one at Farrell High School, back in Bradley. Kien saw three tables on the stage. Two of the tables were set back a little, the third, a very small table no bigger than a desk, had been pushed forward. Chairs were grouped around the tables, and a microphone stood on each. As Kien and the other Vietnamese took their seats, several men and women walked out onto the stage and took their seats at the larger tables. A small, thin man with graying hair sat down at the little table.

"That is Tom Sykes, the Town Moderator," Bill explained to Phat, who translated for Bác Huy. "He will make sure that there is order during the meeting."

Townspeople were now filing in. Kien recognized several fishermen from the pier. With these fishermen came Paul Orrin, who looked over at the Vietnamese community with a smug little smile that Kien didn't like. Orrin knows something is going to happen, he thought.

Bang, bang, bang! Tom Sykes was hammering his table with a small wooden gavel. "This special town meeting will now come to order!" the Moderator called. He banged the gavel some more. "Come to order, folks!"

Bill Ransom eased himself into a seat beside Kien. "Now you'll see a real town meeting, Travor-style," he whispered.

Kien glanced around at the packed auditorium. It was so crowded that people stood crammed into the doorways, jammed against the walls. They all made a lot of noise, but the sound hummed to a silence when Tom Sykes pounded his gavel a third time.

"This special town meeting has been called so that we can hear the recommendations of the Special Committee studying the Vietnamese problem," the Moderator announced. "After we hear the recommendations, we'll vote on them. Because of the seriousness of this matter, we are going to do away with our custom of discussing pending business."

A loud whispering rustled its way around the assembly. Tom Sykes pointed his gavel at the crowd. "Not now, folks! You get to talk afterward, but right now we want to hear from our committee chairwoman, Mary Simmons."

A tall woman got up and pulled the microphone closer. She spread several papers on the desk before her and cleared her throat. "Thanks, Tom. As you know, we've made a thorough study of the problem caused by Vietnamese fishermen in our town. We have looked into several complaints registered by our town fishermen. One of the main complaints is that the Vietnamese charge too little for their catch, and so are able to sell more fish than can other fishermen."

A loud roar erupted from the auditorium. Many

people jumped to their feet and began to shout. Tom
Sykes banged his gavel again.

Slowly the noise subsided. Mary Simmons went on to
list other problems supposedly caused by the Vietnamese. Finally, she said, "Our recommendations are as
follows: Since the Vietnamese are undercutting prices
here in Travor, the Committee feels that they should be
restricted as to the pounds of fish they can sell in a day.
The legal limit would be set by the town, and—"

"What is this 'legal limit'?" Phat was on his feet.
"What you suggest is not lawful!"

Instantly Orrin leaped up. "Sit down, you! A foreigner
isn't going to tell us what to do!"

The gavel banged again and again. "Order!" Tom
Sykes yelled.

But Bill Ransom was also on his feet. "I demand to
hear from the Town Counselor on this matter!" he cried.
"Jim, tell us whether this recommendation is legal or
not."

Tom Sykes turned to a man sitting at one of the larger
tables. "Jim Pinna, you're our Town Counselor. You
heard the question. What do you say?"

A short, elderly man got to his feet. He looked uncomfortable as he said, "As you know, I'm appointed by the
town to look out for Travor's legal rights. I'd have to say
that the recommendation sounds pretty unconstitutional.
I doubt if it would ever hold up in court."

Noise erupted like a volcano. Orrin shook his fist at
the Vietnamese. "What do we care about laws and
courts? I say, we kick these troublemakers out of Travor!"

Phat yelled back, "You are the ones making trouble!
This is our home! We have a right to live where we
choose!"

Above the uproar, Bill Ransom's voice could be heard.
"I'd like to point out something. You people all heard
what the Town Counselor said. Vietnamese came to this
country to live in peace and try to make a living. Is that

so un-American? Seems to me our ancestors did the same thing when they first came here."

Paul Orrin swung around to face Bill across the auditorium. "I've bought a lot of stuff from your Marina, Bill Ransom. Supposing I took my business elsewhere? I don't deal with people who love foreigners more than their own kind. And that goes for the men who work for me, too!"

"You threatening me, Orrin?" Bill thundered.

Paul Orrin threw his arms up into the air. "Look at what these sneaky Vietnamese have done! They undercut our prices. . . . They take away our living. . . . But, worst of all, they turn us against our friends!"

"Let's get rid of them!" someone yelled.

Tom Sykes was trying to restore order, but it wasn't possible. The townspeople were standing, shouting, shaking their fists. Phat grabbed Kien's arm. "We'd better get out of here!" he shouted over the noise. "Stay with Linh! Take care of her!"

Kien got up. His legs felt a little rubbery, and panic rose in him as he smelled the hot hate in the air. Bác Huy was pushing Thuyet ahead of him and leading the way out of the auditorium. Other Vietnamese fell in step behind Kien and Linh. Phat and Bill Ransom drew back, waiting till all the Vietnamese could leave. Kien noticed how pale Phat had become.

"Walk fast, but keep your head up and look them in the eye," Bác Huy ordered over his shoulder. "Kien, Linh, stay close to me."

Kien's heart hammered as he walked through a sea of angry faces. He could hear Paul Orrin's voice yelling behind them. As the Vietnamese tried to leave the auditorium, they were pushed and shoved. Just as most of them had managed to force their way out into the open, Kien heard a roar come from the crowd inside.

"Paul's right! Let's get *rid* of them!"

Push, shove . . . Linh was wrenched away from his side. Kien shouted her name, but could not reach her. Bác Huy turned, trying to reach his daughter. Kien saw someone reach out and shove the little man, hard. Bác Huy lost his footing and fell backward. Someone slammed fists into Phat from behind. Phat fell onto his knees, stunned.

"*Get* them!"

Then Kien saw Linh. She was standing, scared and bewildered, not far away. He started to call to her, saw the bottle sailing through the air, and screamed, "Get down!"

The bottle caught Linh squarely in the back of the head. She crumpled to the ground. As she fell, Kien caught a glimpse of her face, and something in it reminded him of Mai.

Before he could think, he was moving. He ran forward and straddled Linh's fallen body. "You stop!" he shouted at the milling crowd. "You lots brave, throw things at small girl!"

Somehow, Bill Ransom was beside Kien. He picked Linh up in his arms. "I hope you folks are proud of yourselves," he thundered. "Is it American to go around beating up on little kids?"

The crowd stopped, confused. Many men and women turned away. Someone said, "We should be ashamed of ourselves! This is no way to handle things!"

Sirens shrilled above the hubbub. Several policemen came hurrying down the walkway.

"*Now* the police come!" Phat had pushed his way through the crowd to stand with Bill and Kien. "Why were they not here when they were needed?" His normally pleasant face was as fierce as Bác Huy's. "How is Linh?"

Before Bill or Kien could answer, a loud voice called, "The Vietnamese are the ones that caused all this trouble. If they don't want to get hurt, they better stay out of our way!"

Kien saw Bác Huy trying to push through the crowd to get to Orrin. Phat was quicker. "Paul Orrin!" the young man's lips curled back from his teeth in a snarl of rage. Kien had never seen such anger before. "I'll make you pay for this! You'll be sorry!"

Bill grabbed Phat's arm. "You be quiet!" he ordered sternly. "Do you want the riot to start all over again? The important thing is to get Linh and the other kids home. Let's move!"

Bác Huy was already gathering the frightened Vietnamese community together. Kien saw Thuyet take Linh from Bill, saw Phat glaring at Paul Orrin's broad back.

Why did I ever come to this crazy town? Kien wondered. Why?

10

Police seemed to be everywhere, all at once. The Vietnamese had no trouble as they began their walk home. Bác Huy carried Linh, who seemed to have suffered nothing more serious than a headache. Thuyet would not leave her daughter's side, which left Kien to follow with Phat and Bill.

"It was foolish to threaten Orrin like that," Bill told Phat when they had left the school. "I'm surprised at you! I know your uncle is hotheaded, but you're usually very sensible."

Phat's lips tightened. "Orrin can push people just so far," he muttered.

Kien didn't like Phat's expression or his tone of voice. This is definitely not the place for me, he thought. I have nothing to do with these people. Their problems aren't my problems. I must leave Travor as soon as I can, perhaps even tonight!

They walked in silence till they reached the Marina store. Here, Bác Huy formally thanked Bill for his help. "I had not entirely believed my nephew when he said you were our friend," the little leader said. "Now I see that you are. If you hadn't interfered, our people might have been hurt."

When Phat had translated this, Bill Ransom shook his

head. "Kien is the one to thank. He made the crowd ashamed of themselves," he said.

Kien was very embarrassed. He felt even more flustered when Bác Huy and Thuyet began to thank him. "Our daughter is very precious to us," Bác Huy said. "We had two other children, both boys. They were lost at sea. If anything had happened to Linh . . ."

Kien ducked his head. How could he explain to Bác Huy and Thuyet that he had raced to help Linh because of a memory of another girl with long dark hair and clear, brave eyes?

"It wasn't anything," he mumbled.

"It was a courageous thing to do," Bác Huy insisted. The other Vietnamese thought so, too. When they reached their homes at the pier, many of them smiled at Kien in a friendly, even a respectful manner. And when Linh had been put to bed, Thuyet went straight to the kitchen where she began to cook. Soon, delicious smells filled the house.

Kien's mouth watered, but knowing Thuyet, he did not dare ask for any of the food she was making. He was too astonished for words when the gaunt woman brought him a plate piled high with cakes.

"You risked harm to help my Linh," Thuyet told Kien. "I am sorry for the way I've treated you. These cakes are all for you!"

The cakes were delicious. As Kien ate, Thuyet wiped her eyes with the back of her hand.

"Linh is all we have left. You have all our gratitude, Kien, and you will be welcome in this house for as long as you wish to live with us."

She left Kien to finish the cakes and went back to the kitchen. Kien listened to her clattering around and talking to the other women and felt guilty that he was planning to leave. But I have to get out of here tonight, he told himself. There will be trouble, and I don't want to stay around for it!

The moment he thought this, he remembered another night when he had planned to go away. He remembered

Diane, and big Steve Olson, and Tad and Loc, and Mai. Especially Mai. "Oh, Kien," Mai whispered inside his mind. "You are our older brother."

Kien jumped up and walked to the window. He looked out into the darkness to where Bác Huy was sitting on the house step, with Trinh and Phat and several others. As Kien listened, Trinh spoke in a frightened voice.

"Bác Huy, I knew how this meeting would be! I warned you! I've had enough, I can tell you. I'm going to sell my share of the boats, and I am going away. There has to be someplace where my family and I can live in peace."

"All places will be the same," Phat said sternly. "Until we are ready to stand up for our rights, we will never be left in peace."

A woman sniffed. "Stand up for your own rights, then! I agree with Trinh. My husband and I will sell our share of the boats and leave also."

Phat got up abruptly and walked away into the darkness. Kien turned away from the window thinking, I am definitely leaving. This is getting worse and worse.

After some time, Bác Huy came in and went to bed. The others who lived in the house came in also. Slowly, the house settled for sleep. Everyone was so upset that it seemed Kien was the only one to realize that Phat had not come in with the rest. The young man had not returned home when Kien got up softly and slung his airline bag over his shoulder.

I'm sorry I can't say good-by to Phat and Linh, he thought. I wish I could see Bill Ransom, too, but they would all ask me questions or try to make me stay, and I don't want to stay here.

The heavy outer door creaked loudly as Kien opened it. He shivered in the cool night air and for a moment was tempted to take Phat's windbreaker with him. But I cannot do that, Kien told himself. I cannot steal from a friend.

He started down the stairs, and another thought

crossed his mind. He had no money except for a handful
of change. How far would that take him? He hesitated,
half turned back, then shrugged. I will get a ride. I'll
find work . . . and new friends, too! he told himself
resolutely.

The night was clear and full of stars. Kien began to
walk toward the road that led into town. When he had
gone a little way, however, he hesitated. "I will go and
say good-by to the *Seagull*," he murmured. "It might be
some time before I see a fishing town again."

Kien walked toward the pier, swinging his bag. Suddenly, the silence was interrupted by a rattling noise,
followed by a deep, throaty chuckle. Then, footsteps ran
rapidly away from the pier.

"Who's there?" Kien called in English. Silence answered him. Perhaps a fisherman had come to check up
on his boat, Kien thought. Then he saw something
bright flash across the darkness.

"Lightning?" Kien whispered. But it wasn't lightning.
This light didn't go out but became brighter and
brighter. It had a pulsating, flickering quality to it. It
was . . .

"*Lua chay!*" Kien screamed. "Fire! Fire!" He began to
run back toward the Vietnamese community. If the fire
spread, it would burn all the boats moored at the pier.
"Help! Fire!" he yelled.

As he turned a corner, Kien stumbled, ran full tilt into
someone, and almost fell.

"What's going on?" Phat demanded. "Why are you
shouting?"

Kien could do no more than stammer, "It is fire! A
boat's on fire!"

Phat began to run past Kien. He hurried up to the
big house and ran inside, shouting, "A boat is burning!
Hurry, a boat is on fire!"

Bác Huy came rushing out of his house, shirtless and
shoeless. Other men and women poured from the three
houses. "If the fire gets to our boats, we'll be in deep
trouble!" Bác Huy yelled.

The fire was by now leaping into the darkness, casting down showers of sparks. A low moan came from the Vietnamese. Thuyet grabbed Kien. "How did you come to find this fire?" she demanded.

"I was . . . was walking, and I—"

"At this hour! With Orrin's people all around!" Thuyet shook Kien. "You are a troublesome boy! You could have been badly hurt! Now, stand over there, out of harm's way, with Linh!"

Kien had no intention of staying out of harm's way. He ducked under Thuyet's arm and raced out onto the pier after Bác Huy and the others. As he ran, he heard the wail of fire engines. Someone had called the fire department.

"Here come the fire engines!" he shouted, as he pushed in close to Bác Huy and Phat. "The fire engines will put it out!" he called to the Vietnamese who were working to contain the blaze.

Bác Huy spat. "We are only trying to keep our own boats from catching fire. It would be Heaven's justice if this boat burned. It is Orrin's boat!"

Orrin's? Kien stared at the burning boat, then at Phat. An ugly suspicion was starting to tug at his mind. Phat had not been in the house with the others. He had been out walking. Could Phat have chuckled in the darkness as he set fire to the hated Orrin's boat?

"Phat. . . ," Kien began, and the young man turned a cool, blank face toward him. "How do you think this boat caught on fire?" Kien asked.

"How should I know? I was not here," Phat replied calmly. "You saw the fire before I did, didn't you?"

But did I? Kien wondered. Before he could ask any more questions, however, the firemen were among them, pushing back the crowd. If he hadn't been worried about Phat's involvement in all this, Kien would have enjoyed the sounds and the sirens and the red lights that spun around and around on the fire engines. The firemen made short work of the fire, and the flames were smoldering into ash when a big, dark-haired man pushed his way through the crowd to face Phat.

"I want to know how my boat caught on fire!" Orrin roared.

Phat met Paul Orrin's look coolly. "How would I know that?"

"You'd know, all right! You were the one who set fire to my boat and you know it. You threatened to make me sorry, didn't you? Everyone heard you!"

Phat went pale in the red glare of the fire engines. "You are lying."

"No one calls me a liar!" Orrin boomed. "You people stood by while my boat burned. You didn't care if the fire burned up every boat moored by the pier! You threatened me, and you set fire to my boat." He pointed to Bác Huy. "You helped him!"

An ugly rumble of assent rose behind Orrin, and Kien saw most of the American fishermen nodding. Then one of them called, "Get a cop! Arrest that man! He'd have burned up our boats, too, along with Paul's!"

"We have done nothing," Phat cried, but Kien heard the fear in his voice. Am I imagining this? he asked himself. Can Phat have done this thing? It was not like Phat at all, and yet Phat had been terribly angry!

Bác Huy spoke shortly to the other Vietnamese, and they began to elbow their way toward their homes. Orrin and his followers watched them go without trying to stop anyone, but Kien saw Orrin say something to a man nearby. The man nodded and hurried off.

"He is going for the police," Kien whispered to Bác Huy.

The little man looked more fierce than ever. "I am an innocent man and so is Phat. Let them bring their police! What can they do to us?" he cried.

Kien looked at Phat. Say something, Kien pleaded silently. Say you're innocent, too. Phat remained silent.

Wordlessly, they returned to their houses. Thuyet and Linh met them halfway. Thuyet began to scold Kien for running off, then saw her husband's face. "What is wrong?" she cried.

"Orrin's boat was the one on fire," Bác Huy sighed. "He accuses Phat . . . and me!"

"He is crazy!" Thuyet wailed. She grabbed Bác Huy's arm. "What will happen now? What will Orrin do?"

"I don't know. We'd better get into the house," Bác Huy said. The Vietnamese all trooped into Bác Huy's big meeting room and the little leader put his hands to his forehead. Kien saw that Bác Huy's hands were shaking.

Phat took Kien aside. "If the police do come," he whispered, "go to Bill Ransom. He lives in a little house behind the Marina store. Bill will know what to do."

There was a knock on the door. Thuyet's hands leaped up to cover her mouth, but she said nothing. No one moved. No one spoke.

"Police," a voice said. "Mr. Dao, please open up."

Thuyet started toward the door, but Bác Huy got up and gently pushed her aside. He opened the door and pulled himself up to his full height of five feet six inches. Two uniformed policemen stood on the doorstep.

"Huy Dao?" one of them said. Bác Huy nodded. "We want you and your nephew Phat Dao to come down to the station with us. We want to ask you some questions concerning the fire at the pier."

Bác Huy turned questioningly to Phat, who translated. While he was speaking, the second policeman said, "We aren't charging you with anything yet, but a bottle of gasoline and some rags were found near the burned boat. It looks like a case of arson, and that's pretty serious."

Bác Huy pulled back his shoulders. "Tell him that we will go with them," he said in a loud voice. "We have nothing to fear or hide."

The policemen stood aside from the door so that Phat and Bác Huy could walk out of the house. The door closed behind them. Now Thuyet began to wail.

"They've taken my husband and my nephew! What will happen to them?" she sobbed.

Kien was about to say something, when Linh screamed. A rock came smashing through the front window of the house. Glass shattered everywhere.

At the same time, a loud voice in the street below shouted, "Vietnamese, get out of Travor! Get out of town!"

11

"Shut the lights!" Kien shouted. "Get down!"

A second, then a third rock hurtled through the windows. "Arsonists!" the ugly voice in the street yelled. "Get out of Travor before you're run out of town!"

Linh was crying. Kien couldn't tell whether she was hurt or just frightened. He held his breath, waiting for another rock and another shattering of glass, but there was nothing except for the sound of footsteps hurrying away.

"I think they have gone," Trinh's voice said in the darkness. "Is everyone all right?"

Someone turned on the lights. Every window that faced the street had been smashed, and shreds of glass lay all over the floor. One of the women had been cut by the flying glass, and many of the children were crying in fear.

Kien was relieved to see that Linh was unharmed. She ran over to him, saying, "Kien, what shall we do? Will those bad people come again?"

Kien looked down into her frightened eyes and felt scared himself, but he forced a scornful smile. "Of course they won't come back. Now I have to get going. I have to talk to Bill Ransom."

"No one is leaving this house tonight!" Thuyet declared. "I won't let you walk into a trap. Orrin's men may be outside."

Kien had thought of this, too, and he had to keep himself from shivering as he said, "Phat told me to go to Bill's if the police came. He said Bill would know what to do."

"Then let an adult go," Thuyet urged. "Trinh, what about you going for Bill Ransom?"

The thin man was obviously frightened. "As you said yourself, Orrin's men may be outside waiting," he quavered. "A boy might have a better chance of getting through to the Marina store."

Kien didn't wait for any more argument. He hurried to the door and pulled it open. It was very dark outside, and he hesitated until he heard Linh whisper, "Kien, don't! I . . . I don't want you to get hurt." If somebody doesn't go for help, Kien thought, we might all end up getting hurt.

He slipped down the steps and onto the road that led to town. Glancing up at the stars, Kien noted that the North Star glittered steadfast in the sky. For some reason, the thought of that constant star comforted him, and he remembered a gentle old man who had taught him about the stars and the sea.

"Grandfather," he whispered, "I wish you were here now. This whole world has gone crazy."

The streets were deserted, but fear of Orrin's men kept Kien's heart pounding all the way into the center of town. When at last he reached Bill's Marina store, Kien could hardly breathe. Bill was fast asleep in his house behind the store, and it was some moments before he answered Kien's urgent knocking.

Bill blinked when he saw who was standing at the door. "Kien!" Then he asked, "What happened?"

Kien gasped out the story in a few words. "Phat said I must find you, police come," he explained. "They take him, Bác Huy, police station. People come, throw rocks."

"Come in. It'll take me a few seconds to get dressed."

Kien hurried inside the house. "Then you and I will go to the police station and see what's going on."

Kien sat down on a chair in Bill's small living room. It was a pleasant little room, decorated with shells and coral and other objects from the sea. Kien noticed a photograph on the wall that showed Bill with an older man and woman.

"My parents," Bill explained, coming back into the room. "They live in another part of California. What about your family, Kien?"

"Not alive," Kien said. "I no have family."

Bill frowned. "I thought you came to Travor looking for your relatives!" Kien's cheeks began to grow hot. He had forgotten that lie! "Okay, Kien," Bill said "I think you'd better tell me the real story."

"Bác Huy . . . Phat . . . needing us," Kien said urgently, but Bill sat down across from Kien.

"They'll wait for us. I don't like being lied to, Kien, and I have a feeling you haven't told me the truth. Now, let's have it."

Bill's eyes and voice were very stern. Kien sighed and sketched the story of his arrival in Hong Kong, the refugee camp, the Olsons' home. "Is not for me," Kien said. "Mai and Loc, they happy. Better without me. Anyway, I want see America, have adventure. I remember Phat from plane, so I come here."

"So that's how it is." Bill's voice became sterner than before. "Where were you going when you spotted the fire tonight, eh? Getting ready to run away from Travor?"

"Not understand," Kien stammered.

"I think you do. There's an expression in America which says, 'Rats desert a sinking ship.' You were going to run off because things were getting hard to handle in Travor. You were going to go off without a thought for your friends."

Kien said nothing, but he felt angry and a little ashamed. It wasn't that way, he wanted to shout at Bill. I wasn't deserting anyone! Yet, it was true that he had meant to leave because of the trouble.

Bill said in a softer tone, "Well, at least you didn't run off when you saw the fire. And you came looking for me tonight, which was a brave thing to do. Are you brave enough to come to the police station with me? Or do you want me to drop you off on the road leading out of Travor?"

The thought had been in Kien's mind, but now he shook his head. "I will go with you," he snapped. "I not run away!"

Bill smiled. "Good," was all he said, but Kien knew that the man was no longer angry with him. "My motorcycle is parked in back. We'll take that."

They rode away from Bill's house in the lonely night. The streets they passed were deserted and still, but by the glow of streetlights Kien glimpsed the outlines of fine homes, trees, and gardens. "Travor is a pretty town," Bill called over his shoulder. "It'll be a fine place to live once this trouble is over."

But will it ever be over? Kien wondered. He clung to Bill's broad back in silence, wondering whether Orrin and men like him would ever let the trouble die down. They hate us, Kien thought. But why?

Then, a quiet voice seemed to speak in his tired mind. "Kien, men act evilly because they are afraid. Deep down, Orrin and his friends are afraid of the Vietnamese. It is the fear that makes them act so."

Kien blinked and shook his head to clear it. That was what Grandfather would have said, if he were alive. The gentle old teacher had hated no one and refused to do evil to anyone. But then, Teacher Van Chi had never met Paul Orrin!

"There's the police station," Bill said, pointing. He rode his motorcycle to the curb and parked it. "Let's go and see what's happened to Huy and Phat."

Kien followed Bill into the police station. As soon as they were inside, they saw Bác Huy. He looked angry and bewildered, as he talked in Vietnamese to a policeman who sat behind a desk.

"Bác Huy!" Kien cried. "Are you all right?"

Bác Huy's tired face lighted up when he saw Kien and Bill. "I am all right. They are letting me go! But they are keeping Phat here. Come and tell this policeman to let Phat go, too!" he cried.

"Keeping Phat?" Bill repeated, when Kien had translated Bác Huy's words. He turned to the policeman behind the desk. "What's going on here? Have you charged Phat Dao with something?"

"He's been charged with arson," the policeman replied. Kien's heart sank.

Bác Huy burst out, "They say that Phat set the fire to Orrin's boat. How could this be? Phat was in the house with all of us. He told me so!"

Kien automatically translated these words for Bill, but he felt terribly depressed. Phat was lying. Why lie, unless he had started the fire?

Learning that it had been Kien who had spotted the fire first, the policeman asked him many questions. Kien, hoping to shield Phat, said nothing about the sounds he had heard just before the fire started. It was useless.

"Phat Dao's fingerprints were found on the bottle of gasoline we found near the fire," the police officer told Bill and Kien. "A lot of people heard him threaten Paul after the town meeting. Sounds like a clear-cut case of revenge to me."

"Can we see Phat?" Bill asked. The policeman unlocked a steel-barred door that led to two cells in the back of the police station. In one of these cells, Phat sat with his head in his hands. He looked up when Bác Huy, Kien, and Bill hurried up, and his face was as pale as ashes.

"Don't worry, Phat," Bill said. "I know a good lawyer. We'll get you out of here in no time."

Bill had spoken in English, but Bác Huy understood. "You must not be afraid, my nephew! You are innocent!" he cried.

Phat shook his head slowly. "It's no use," he groaned. "Don't you see? Orrin is too strong. He'll win. He always wins!"

12

When they returned home, Kien and Bác Huy were exhausted. Thuyet began to question them, but Bác Huy held up his hand. "Phat is still being held by the police," he told his wife and the others. "I'll tell you everything later, but right now I'm going to bed. I'm so tired I can hardly stand up."

Kien was just as weary and lay down on his mat without bothering to change into nightclothes. Still, he couldn't sleep. He kept remembering the crackle and roar the flames made as they leaped up against the dark night. He remembered other sounds, too—that chuckle, the running footsteps. Had they been made by Phat? He was still trying to puzzle this out when he finally dozed off.

"Kien! Kien! Wake up! There's trouble at the pier!"

Kien sprang awake to Linh's voice. Dazed and half asleep, he blinked at Linh, who had been running and was all out of breath.

"What happened?" he demanded.

"We were kept home from school this morning because of the trouble yesterday. I was with Mother at the pier. She sent me to get Father," Linh panted. "Orrin's men were waiting when our fishermen came in with their catch. They stood around the scales and watched our men weigh their fish. Then they allowed us to sell only a small portion of the catch. They threw the rest back into the seal When we protested, they began to push us around."

Bác Huy came awake instantly. "I'm going down to the pier," he cried. "Kien, you and Linh stay here!"

As the little man ran out of the house, Linh clenched her small fists. "I hate these people!" she cried. "They treat us as if we were animals. They are evil, all of them!"

"No . . . they're afraid." Linh stared at him and Kien felt a bit embarrassed as he tried to explain. "My grandfather used to say that people weren't evil, just afraid. These people in Travor are afraid we'll take away their way of making a living."

"Why should anyone be afraid of us?" Linh protested. "That's silly!"

Kien shook his head. "I don't know," he admitted, and a sudden loneliness for the old teacher clamped around his heart. I wish you were here now, Teacher Van Chi, he thought. We could certainly use your advice!

Linh sniffed. "Well, I'm not going to sit around here and wait. Are you?" With a flash of braids, she ran out of the front door. Kien followed, catching up with her halfway to the pier. From this distance they could see that a large group of people had gathered, and Kien could hear Orrin shouting.

"We're just upholding the recommendation made by the Special Committee," Orrin was booming. "By making sure that you Vietnamese can only sell a set portion of fish each day, we're protecting our own way of making a living!"

"Not lawl" Kien heard Bác Huy yell back in English. Kien pushed and shoved till he was standing next to the little leader. "Tell this one that what he does is unlawful," Bác Huy cried.

Kien translated. There was a little stir in the crowd around them. Kien saw that it was an uneasy stir. "You know, Paul, he's got a point," one of the fishermen said.

"The recommendation never came up for a vote. And when Bill Ransom asked whether it'd hold up in court our Town Counselor wasn't so sure—"

"Maybe we could get into trouble doing this," another fisherman chipped in.

Kien played on their uncertainty. "Bad thing! Not law!" he cried. "Men fish all day, you put fish back in sea. Is American to do?"

Heads started to nod, and one or two men left the circle around Orrin and began to walk away. Seeing that he was losing his following, Paul Orrin raised his voice. "Who's this little foreigner to tell us what's American and what isn't? We're the Americans here!" he cried. "It's still our country, isn't it?"

The fishermen halted, looking uncertain. Paul Orrin said to Kien in a low voice, "Boy, if you don't want to get hurt, stay out of my way! Phat Dao's in jail. Make sure you don't join him!"

Bác Huy couldn't understand everything that Orrin had said, but he picked up Phat's name. Eyes blazing, he moved in on the big man. "What does Orrin say about Phat?" he demanded.

Kien had no chance to translate this question. Orrin cried, "Does this little creep want to fight me?" He reached out, grabbing Huy by the shoulders and hoisting him up in the air.

He got more than he bargained for. With his feet dangling in midair, Bác Huy aimed a punch at Orrin that made the big man stagger backward. Orrin dropped Bác Huy. "Hit me, will you?"

As if this was a signal, everything exploded. Orrin's supporters ran forward. So did the Vietnamese. Thuyet and the other women began to scream, and Kien heard someone cry, "Get the police! Get the police!"

He himself was sandwiched between a heap of smelly fish and a mass of fighting bodies. Dodging a blow, Kien was shoved right into the pile of fish. By the time he had managed to scramble out of the slippery mess, the fight was over.

Police sirens cut through the shouting and the screaming, and police officers quickly broke things up. No one seemed badly hurt, but Kien could see black eyes and bloody noses, and hating faces. "This isn't over," Orrin growled at Bác Huy. "You asked for trouble, Huy Dao. Now you'll really get it!"

The police ordered everyone home, and closed the pier for the remainder of the day. Police officers were posted to see that this order was carried out. Kien watched the fishermen, both Vietnamese and American, move away from the pier, and thought, Closing the pier is a mistake. Now all the men will stay home rather than go out to sea. They will talk and start hating each other more and more.

Kien was right. Though dispersed by police order, the American fishermen did not leave the area. They gathered in groups and stood around talking. Sometimes they would stare toward the Vietnamese houses, as if making plans. When they saw any Vietnamese, they shouted, "Why don't you get out of Travor? We don't want your kind around!"

In the midst of all this, Bill Ransom came roaring down the street on his motorcycle. He got plenty of black looks, and there was some name-calling. Bill ignored all this and went straight to Bác Huy's house.

"Phat was arraigned this morning in district court," he told the Vietnamese. He explained that Phat, along with a lawyer, had gone before a judge to plead innocent to the charge of arson. "Because of the troubled situation in Travor, the judge set Phat's bail very high. Otherwise, he said, Phat might be released on bail and come back to Travor to set more fires."

Kien translated. Bác Huy was outraged. "Phat never set fire to Orrin's boat! Why would he set new fires?" he cried.

"He is being held at the county jail in the next town until trial," Bill went on. "Perhaps it is the safest place for him to be. If he was out on bail, Orrin's men might try to hurt him. The mood's turning ugly in this town."

Kien felt a shiver of fear. "What can we do, Bill?"

"Stay home. Lock the doors and don't go near the windows. If you need to go out of your homes, go in groups." He dropped a hand on Kien's shoulder. "I was wrong to lecture you last night. This really isn't your fight. If you want a ride out of town, I'll take you now."

Kien was tempted. Then he looked at Bác Huy and Linh and shook his head. He could not run away. "I stay," he said.

The approval in Bill's eyes made Kien stand a little straighter. "Nothing will happen, probably. There are police stationed at the pier, and many more will be patrolling this area looking for signs of trouble. Even so, be careful. Now I have to get back to the Marina."

After Bill's motorcycle had roared away, Kien's brief pride disappeared. What's the matter with me? he wondered. I should have gone with him. Now it is too late to leave Travor!

When Kien told Bác Huy all that Bill had said, the little man looked even more fierce and determined. "We will call a meeting of all the community," he said. "They should hear what has been said."

Kien was sent from house to house to call the fishermen and their families to a meeting. All of them crammed into Bác Huy's big room and listened to what he had to say. When the little man had finished, Trinh spoke up.

"Bác Huy, my family and I are packing. Will you buy my share of the boats?" he asked. "We want to leave Travor as soon as possible."

Another man nodded, and his wife said, "Life is too precious. We left our homes before we came to America, and we will leave this place, too. We'll find some place else to live!"

Several other Vietnamese agreed with Trinh. Bác Huy said that he couldn't stop anyone from leaving and arranged to pay them for their share of the fishing boats. When the meeting was over, he turned to his family and sighed.

"Perhaps they are right. I can't blame anyone for wanting to leave this place. Once it was a paradise, a place where we thought to live by our work, raise our children in peace. Now living here is becoming a nightmare!"

Thuyet said sharply, "Nightmare or not, this is our home. No one will move me from this house. I'd like to see anyone try it!"

"So would I, Aunt," Kien said, with a trace of his old impudence. It produced a small laugh that broke the tension.

Bác Huy had instructed everyone to go home, stay indoors, and keep an eye out for Orrin's men. As the Vietnamese silently left for their homes, Bác Huy shook his head sadly. "Now you will see. It begins," he said.

The afternoon turned to twilight, then evening. Thuyet and the other women cooked a meal in silence. They ate in the same silence, listening, wondering what the night would bring. The silence and the waiting made Kien uneasy. Orrin is sure to start something, he kept thinking. The question is what . . . and when?

Probably because of the increased police patrols in the area, nothing happened at first. Bác Huy's household even went to bed as if this were an ordinary night. Then, around three in the morning, Kien started awake. Had he imagined he'd heard running footsteps?

No, he had not! There was a splintering crash, followed by many others as rocks were thrown through the windows of the three Vietnamese houses. There were no shouts, no cries, only the swiftly running feet, the rain of stones, the shards of glass all over everything. In the dark, heavy silence a child whimpered.

"Is everyone all right?" Bác Huy called softly.

"We are safe," someone replied, and Kien heard the little leader whisper, "That is just the beginning."

But the dawn came without further rock-throwing. The only evidence of hate the Vietnamese found when they left their homes the next morning was the "WAIT" painted on the steps and sidewalk.

Bác Huy looked at the word uncertainly. "They threaten us. Is it wise to go out to sea this morning?" he wondered.

"Perhaps they want us to stay home," one of the men said uncertainly. "They want us to stop fishing. They would like to see us starve!"

Bác Huy thought about this and decided, "We'll go out to sea as usual, then. However, we'll bring the boats in earlier than usual. All women and children must stay inside the houses till we return."

Kien spent the morning cleaning up splinters of glass and boarding up the windows with old wood. "This reminds me of the war," he told Linh. "The war back in Vietnam."

Linh sighed. "It isn't a war. It's just that horrible Orrin and his men. Kien, I'm so tired of staying inside the house. No one is on the street. Can't we play outside on the porch?"

"You heard what your father said—no one is allowed out," Kien said, but he, too, looked yearningly onto the sunlit street and the sea beyond. It was a hot day, and the air inside the house was especially stifling. "Well," he finally agreed, "maybe we can stay on the porch."

When they saw Kien and Linh, other children came out of their homes. At first, they all stayed around their porches, afraid to venture far. But everything looked peaceful, and they decided to play a quick game of tag on the street. Linh joined the game, but Kien sat down on the porch to watch. It was a good thing he did, for he spotted a group of youths running swiftly down the street toward the Vietnamese children.

"Look out!" Kien yelled. "Get back to the houses!"

As he cried out, high school age boys armed with baseball bats and hockey sticks came running down the street. They scattered the playing children and began to hit indiscriminately. Kien saw one little boy go down and was off the porch and running. "Stop!" he shouted in English. "Stop this!"

Thuyet and the other women now came running out

of the houses. Thuyet had a broom in her hands, and as
she ran down the steps she brandished it over her head.
Reaching the nearest youths, she began to beat them
with the broom, shouting all the while in Vietnamese.

"Your mothers should be ashamed! Cowards and
wicked boys, to hurt little children! I'll teach you
manners."

The other women now joined the fight, and soon the
teenagers decided that they had enough and ran away.
Kien, who had been knocked on the head with the butt
end of a hockey stick, now sat up and grinned at
Thuyet.

"Aunt," he said, "if you went after Paul Orrin like
that, I'm sure he'd leave us alone!"

The light of battle still blazed in Thuyet's eyes. "I will
hit him with this broom when I see him," she declared.
Then she frowned. "But, look. Isn't that Bác Huy and
the others? What are they doing home so early?"

Bác Huy and the other fishermen looked dejected.
They walked with their shoulders hunched over, heads
bowed. "No gas," Bác Huy told the women. "They won't
sell us gas for our boats. When we brought what little
we were able to catch in to shore, Orrin's men had
scared away our usual customers. They are determined
not to let us make our living here."

Thuyet's face became very pale. "What shall we do?"

"What can we do? We shall wait," Bác Huy sighed.
He brushed past Thuyet and went into his house.
Thuyet followed, her head bowed. Linh came up to
Kien, her eyes blazing.

"Do you still say that these people are afraid of us?"
she asked scornfully. "I say they are evil!" Kien couldn't
think of a thing to say.

Evening fell again. Around nine o'clock, a woman's
voice began to scream, *"Lua chay! Lua chay!"*

Fire! Kien leaped to pull open the door and look outside. One of the three Vietnamese houses was burning.
Bác Huy and Thuyet, Kien and Linh ran out to try to
put out the flames. But, by the time the fire engines

came and got the fire under control, the house had been badly damaged.

Luckily, no one had been hurt in the fire. The three families who had lived in this house came to stay with Bác Huy and his household, but only temporarily. "We lost much in the fire, but we are unhurt," they told the little leader. "Tomorrow night we may not be so lucky. We are following Trinh's example and we are getting out of Travor."

Bác Huy bowed his head and said nothing, but Thuyet began to cry. "It is a bitter life under Heaven," she sobbed. "A bitter life!"

Kien remembered how Lam had cried back in the refugee camp. She cried because she couldn't come to America, he said to himself. She should have been grateful! He couldn't bear to sit by and listen to Thuyet's grief and went to sit in a corner of the dark hall by himself. After a while, Linh came to sit with him. She said nothing, and Kien understood how she felt. After a long silence, Linh whispered, "When we first came here, I thought I had never seen such a lovely place as Travor."

Kien reached out and gave her hand a squeeze. It was cold in spite of the muggy heat.

"You don't know how bad it was for us in Vietnam," Linh went on in a low voice. "My father was a well-to-do fisherman in our village, but the New Government taxed us and taxed us, and we couldn't live on what we were allowed to keep for ourselves. There were five of us, then. Mother, Father, my two little brothers . . ."

A silence fell between them, and Kien knew she was thinking of those little boys, lost at sea. The sea was cruel, devouring what it could. No, that wasn't right, either. A sea was not wicked. People were wicked. Outside, a voice shouted, "Go home, Vietnamese! We don't want you around here!"

Where is home? Kien wondered. Wherever it is, we are far away from it. That much is sure.

"We were at sea for weeks and weeks," Linh began again. "When we finally washed up on the coast of

Malaysia, the government didn't want to take us in. They almost pushed us back out to sea. At last we were allowed to go to a refugee camp." Linh's voice was very low. "We lived in that camp for nine months. And then, we came to America! We were so grateful to get here that when we landed, Father got down on his knees and knocked his forehead on the earth to thank Heaven for bringing us to safety."

Kien said nothing. The night was quiet with a heavy stillness, a waiting silence. "Kien, what will happen to us?" Linh was asking. "If Father and the other men can't fish, how will we live? We'll have to leave, won't we? Where could we go?"

"Try and get some rest," Kien said. He felt helpless and angry and sad at the same time. Orrin was winning, and there was nothing he or anyone else could do about it. "I think the worst is over for now. Nothing more will happen tonight."

"But there's always tomorrow, isn't there?" Linh said. "I wonder what will happen tomorrow."

13

The day dawned sluggish, gray, and oppressive. When Kien awoke he felt a strangeness in the house, and then he realized that Bác Huy and the other men were still at home. No one had gone out to sea.

"Last night," Kien murmured, remembering. The night hung behind him like a heavy black curtain, full of fear and hopelessness. He got up and went to the door, opened it to look out. The street was empty, but the charred house reminded him of the fire. "Orrin probably was behind that fire," he muttered to himself. "Only, of course, we'll never be able to prove it."

Bác Huy was sitting in the small kitchen when Kien came inside again. "Last night was nothing," he said, his fierce eyes tired and red-rimmed from lack of sleep. "Orrin will think up new ways to harass and hurt us."

"We can't sit back and do nothing!" Thuyet grumbled, placing a fresh pot of tea on the rickety kitchen table.

"No, you are right." Bác Huy took a deep breath. "I will go and talk with Orrin."

"What can be gained by talking with such a monster!" Thuyet protested, and Linh, who had come into the kitchen, shook her head wildly.

"Father, you mustn't go! Orrin will hurt you!"

At this moment, there was a loud knock on the door.

The Vietnamese stared at one another. "I will see who it is," Kien said.

He ran to the door and peered through the keyhole. It was Orrin! There was no mistaking the big man. Kien raced back to the kitchen.

"What is the matter with you?" Thuyet demanded. "You are trembling!"

"Orrin is out there," Kien stammered. "He is standing in front of the door."

Bác Huy got up. He gave a determined hitch to his trousers. "I will go speak with him," he said. "Linh, stay here with your mother. Kien, come and translate what I have to say."

They both walked to the front door together, and Bác Huy flung open the door. Orrin was standing on the doorstep alone, but on the street below waited several fishermen who worked for him.

"I want to talk to you, Dao," he said to Bác Huy.

Kien felt a huge dislike for Orrin. The man was smoking a pipe, and the fragrance of it curled around his head and drifted up toward the shuttered windows. He looked rested and confident, as if he knew he would get what he wanted.

"Talk," Bác Huy agreed grimly.

"You're not going to invite me in? That's a pity. I thought we could discuss this matter like businessmen. I heard you've been having a bit of trouble here lately."

Bác Huy's lips formed a tight smile as Kien translated. "A little," he agreed.

"I've got to hand it to you. You're a hard man to scare, Dao. I hear a lot of your people have left, screaming, for the hills."

Bác Huy's hands went to fists. "Say what you have to say, Orrin, then get out!" he snapped.

"All right. I'm going to make you an offer."

"An offer to have us leave Travor?"

"Yes, but I'll sweeten the deal." Orrin took the pipe stem from his mouth and gestured with it toward the pier. "I'm going to offer you a decent price for your

share of the boats, Huy Dao. Also, I'm going to drop
charges against your nephew. If you agree to my terms,
I'll post bond for Phat today. He'll be out of jail within
the hour. Then, I'll tell the District Attorney that I no
longer want to take Phat to trial."

Bác Huy frowned. "Can he do this?" he asked.

"So he says. He says that he will set Phat free."

Bác Huy frowned. Then he shook his head. "Well, I
cannot do what he asks, even for Phat! After all, my
nephew is innocent. I don't need Paul Orrin to free him.
The courts will do so!"

Kien did not translate these words. Instead, he tugged
at Bác Huy's arm. "Before you refuse Orrin's offer, perhaps you should talk to Phat," he said, under his breath.

Bác Huy looked searchingly at Kien. "What are you
saying?" he demanded. "Is there something you haven't
told me about Phat?"

Kien nodded. Unhappily he told Bác Huy about the
chuckle he had heard, the running footsteps, and then
his meeting with Phat. "He lied to you, Bác Huy. He
wasn't asleep in the house as he told you. I met him outside, near the pier," Kien finished.

Orrin drew pipe smoke into his mouth, blew it out. "If
I were you, Dao, I'd accept this offer. You don't have
much of a choice. The town hates you, and you'll soon
be starved out or . . . worse."

Kien translated. Bác Huy groaned. "Tell him that I
want to think this offer over. We will meet him at the
county jail where Phat is being held. Tell him to meet us
there in an hour."

When Orrin had gone, the little leader closed his eyes
and slumped against the wall. Kien felt terrible, but he
didn't know what to say or do.

"My nephew lied," Bác Huy muttered. "He lied to me
and to the police. Even so, I can't believe that he would
set fire to Orrin's boat. Not Phat!"

Thuyet and Linh had been listening in horror. "Will
you really sell that man our share of the boats?" Thuyet
now asked.

Bác Huy looked like a cornered animal. "I may have to. If Phat is guilty, Orrin wins. If I sell my share, the others in the community will do so, also. We'll all have to leave Travor."

Linh stared to cry. Bác Huy, looking as if he too wanted to cry, nodded to Kien, and both of them left the house. "We will go to see Bill Ransom," Bác Huy decided, once they were outside. "If Phat is in real trouble, Bill may be able to advise us."

But Bill had his own problems. When they reached his Marina store, they found Bill outside sweeping glass from his smashed store window and trying to clean off signs that had been painted all over his store walls.

"A bunch of no-goods broke into my store last night and smashed up some stuff," he told Kien angrily. Kien noted a sign that read, "Gook Lover," on one of the Marina walls and thought, Orrin is punishing Bill for siding with us. Now the Vietnamese will have fewer friends than ever.

Since Bill could not leave his store, Kien and Bác Huy alone took a bus to the county jail where Phat was being held. As they rode the bus, Kien was aware that the sky was turning dark with storm clouds. The skies were nothing compared to Bác Huy's face, however, when they reached the jail and asked to speak with Phat.

It was the first time Kien had seen Phat since his arrest. Dark circles hollowed Phat's eyes, and he looked thinner. Bác Huy, however, didn't ask about Phat's health. Instead, he told his nephew about Orrin's offer.

"Orrin says that he will free you if I agree to sell my share of the boats," he said bluntly. "Now, I need the truth from you. Are you the man who set fire to Orrin's boat?"

Phat bowed his head. "My uncle, I will tell you the truth. I was going to do so," he said in a low voice. "I was furious at Orrin for what he was doing to us. I . . . I got some gasoline and put it into a bottle and took some rags. I was going to burn one of Orrin's boats. But when I got to the pier, someone had already set fire to Orrin's boat!"

"So you are *not* guilty!" Kien cried.

Bác Huy shook his head. "It doesn't matter. Don't you see? The police found the bottle of gasoline. They will say Phat is guilty anyway." He groaned. "Phat will be put into prison or . . . or deported."

The young man buried his face in his hands. "I am ashamed," he said. "I was insane, thinking of setting fire to a boat."

Kien looked at Bác Huy, but the little man seemed not to have heard. He drew a deep breath that sounded like a sob. "Orrin will have his way," he said. "I will accept his offer."

A policeman now came in. "Mr. Dao? A Paul Orrin is waiting to see you," he said.

It seemed to Kien that Bác Huy shrank, grew smaller, as he stood up. His voice cracked, but he tried to speak bravely. "I will go and see him. Come, Kien."

Paul Orrin looked cheerful and full of confidence. He had a man with him, whom he introduced as a bail bondsman. "As soon as we finish with the business of the boats, Phat will be free on bail," he assured Bác Huy. "As I promised, I will also drop all charges against him."

"Then, when I sign the paper, Phat will be freed?" Bác Huy asked in a dull voice.

Orrin nodded. He placed a legal-looking document on a desk. "Tell Dao to sign his name here," he instructed Kien.

Kien noted that Orrin seemed to be purring, like a big, contented cat. He frowned. Why was Orrin so happy? True, he was finally getting the Vietnamese out of Travor, but in order to do so, he had been forced to free Phat. Phat was supposedly the one who had burned Orrin's boat. Didn't Orrin care about the boat at all?

"Tell him to release Phat. I will sign," Bác Huy sighed.

He leaned forward to sign the paper. Orrin leaned forward, too. As the little Vietnamese signed his name, Orrin chuckled deep in his throat.

Kien felt as if someone had sent an electric shock through every part of his body. He stood there, staring at Orrin. That chuckle . . . He had heard that chuckle on the night Orrin's boat was burned! He remembered clearly the chuckle, and the running footsteps.

Now Kien knew why the big man was pleased. He also knew who had set fire to Orrin's boat. Paul Orrin had set fire to it himself!

14

"Stop, Bác Huy! Don't sign!" But Kien was too late. Orrin picked up the sales agreement, and then, smiling, he put a cashier's check on the desk in front of Bác Huy.

"You're getting a fair price, Dao. I'm now going to see the other members of your community. I'm sure they'll be reasonable now that you've sold out."

Kien didn't translate this remark. He didn't have to. Bác Huy knew what would happen, even better than Orrin. Without a word he picked up the check and stuffed it into his pocket. "Let us get Phat and go home," he told Kien.

At that moment, Phat was led into the room. Bác Huy at once turned to his nephew, but Kien stood looking at Orrin. He hated this cruel, cunning man and yet he was fascinated by him. "It is wrong, what you do," he began.

Orrin made a rude noise. "Run along, sonny," he said. "I've finished doing business with you and your friends."

Kien could hardly speak, knowing what he knew. "I know what you do, Mr. Orrin. You set fire to boat, not Phat. I know!"

For a second, Orrin's deep-set eyes narrowed. Then he laughed. "You're crazy, boy," he said.

"Not crazy! I hear you that night—" But before Kien

could say any more, Orrin reached out and grabbed him, hard, by the shoulder.

"Sonny, if you open your mouth once more, I'll have you in jail for spreading lies!" He leaned closer, adding softly, "And if you think you can prove what you just said, forget it! I'm a big man here in Travor. What I say here goes. You come anyplace near to me again, and I'll make sure you never forget it. Now, get out!"

Kien went. Rage filled him, making it hard for him to breathe as he hurried over to Phat and Bác Huy. The little man gave him a blind look. "Let us go," he whispered.

They went. Bác Huy walked as if in a dream, and Phat stumbled along beside him. Neither looked up to notice how much darker the sky now was, but Kien felt that the air around them was heavy and sultry with a brewing storm. The rain was holding off, but Kien could hear thunder rolling in the distance.

"It will storm," Bác Huy said in a listless voice. "It is a good thing our boats did not put out to sea."

"Our boats." Phat hung his head, and tears began to roll down his cheeks. "Uncle, I am sorry. So sorry."

Should I tell them what I know about Orrin? Kien wondered. No. What good would it do? There is no way to prove anything. We have no chance against him. We never did have a chance against him.

Dispiritedly, they trudged along and took a bus back to town. They didn't speak to one another at all. Kien did not know what the others were thinking, but he himself knew what he would do. I will move on, he thought. I will start another adventure somewhere. The thought did not cheer him up.

A dazzling flash of lightning now forked through the sky, followed by a peal of thunder. The storm was getting nearer. As the bus left them in Travor, Kien noted that the skies were darker than before.

"We'd better hurry or we'll get caught in the downpour," he urged Phat and Bác Huy. Neither of the men paid any attention.

They trudged through the town, past Bill Ransom's battered Marina store, past groups of people who were standing together, watching the Vietnamese. Kien knew that the townspeople realized that the Vietnamese were beaten.

You deserve Orrin, Kien wanted to tell them. Sooner or later, Orrin would cheat Travor as he had cheated the Vietnamese.

More lightning flashed through the sky, and the thunder was much closer as they left the town and walked toward the sea. Still the rain held off. They were almost at Wilshire Street, when, suddenly, a dazzling stab of light arced against the now inky sky. At the same instant, a boom of thunder made Kien clap his hands over his ears.

"That was the closest yet!" he cried.

Neither Bác Huy nor Phat paid any attention to the thunderclap. Phat pointed to a car parked near the pier. "Orrin is here," he commented.

"Of course. He told me that he would lose no time," Bác Huy replied grimly. "By now I am sure he has bought all the boats that once belonged to us."

Phat started to speak, but a shout from Orrin interrupted him. "Help!" Orrin was bellowing. "Help! Fire!"

At the same instant, Kien saw a tongue of orange flame shoot up from one of the larger boats on the water.

"That's one of Orrin's boats!" Bác Huy cried. "The lightning must have struck a mast and set the craft on fire!"

Kien started to run forward, but Phat stopped him. "Where are you going?" he demanded. "That boat is Orrin's. Let him take care of his own fire."

Phat's eyes were dark and hating. Kien did not like the look in them. That look reminded him of Sim Evans, and of Orrin himself.

"Let us get closer," Phat said softly. "I want to see Orrin's face as he watches his property burn!"

Now the Vietnamese were pouring out of their homes.

Nobody moved to help Orrin. Instead, they stood watching. "Orrin came to us a little while ago and bought all of our shares in the boats," one man told Bác Huy. "This is Heaven's justice."

He had spoken in Vietnamese, but Orrin seemed to understand that no one was going to help him. Desperately he whirled around and faced the Vietnamese. "Help me put out this fire!" he cried. No one moved. "I'll give a hundred dollars to anyone who helps me!"

"I would not help you for a million dollars, Mr. Orrin." And Phat spat on the ground.

Kien felt something cold and frightening move against his spine. Sim Evans had spat on the ground like that!

Orrin saw the hard faces watching him and gave a shout of fury. He raced to the blazing boat and, pulling off his jacket, began to beat at the fire. Phat laughed.

"What do you expect to do? Fan the flames higher?" he taunted.

The fire was strong and stubborn. A wind whipping out of the still rainless sky fanned the flames into orange arms that reached out for Orrin. Kien saw the big man stagger back, coughing and shielding his face with his arms. Then he staggered forward again, trying to beat out the flames.

"Help me!" he screamed.

No one moved. Thuyet cried. "You were behind the mob that hurt my Linh! I hope you burn with your boat!"

Now the wind was whirling away pieces of burning wood from the boat. The bits of wood fell into the sea, hissing and sizzling as though in anger. Then a very large chunk of blazing wood was swirled up and away from the fire. As Kien watched, it fell toward Orrin.

"Look! Something has hit Orrin!" Linh cried.

Orrin crumpled slowly. He did not fall backward out of danger, but toward the fire. "The man will be burned!" Kien cried out.

No one moved. Bác Huy whispered, "Then let him burn! He urged the mobs to stone our houses. They set fire to one of our homes. This man has done evil. This is justice."

Suddenly, a quiet thought formed in Kien's mind. That man is still a man. He may have done evil, but he is human. If you do not help him, he will die.

That was what Grandfather Van Chi would have done. Old and shaking, Grandfather would have gone to Orrin's aid. Kien started forward. He could not seem to help himself.

"Kien!" Linh screamed. "No! Don't go!"

Kien reached Orrin. He grabbed the big man around the waist and tugged, but could not budge him. Orrin was too heavy! Flames swirled around them both, and Kien coughed, gagging on the smoke.

He wanted to cry out for help, but could not. Smoke filled his nose and throat and lungs, and the flames were singeing his eyebrows and hair. Only his mind could cry out, and he sent one thought into the flames and his own fear.

I can't do it, Grandfather! If no one helps me, I'll burn along with him.

Then something hit Kien squarely in the back, and he crumpled down on top of Paul Orrin's still body. In the moment before he pitched from smoke and flame to darkness, Kien thought he saw the old teacher's face. I must be dying, he thought, and then that thought, too, was lost.

15

"Kien . . . Kien! Kien, please wake up!"

There was noise and confusion all around him. He could hear a loud siren, shouting, and the sound of running feet. His eyelids felt heavy, and it was a struggle to get them open, but when he did, he found Linh kneeling beside him.

"Oh, Kien!" She clapped her hands in relief. "You're all right! When they dragged you away from the fire, you weren't moving, and I was so afraid."

Kien frowned, trying to remember what had happened. Then he thought of Orrin, the lightning, the fire on the boat. "Orrin?" he asked Linh.

Thuyet, who was kneeling beside Linh, answered. "He is safe, thanks to Phat and Bác Huy, who dragged both of you away from the fire." She paused. "If you hadn't gone after him, no one would have moved a finger to save Orrin's life!"

I know that, Kien thought. He ached all over, from his head to his lungs, and there was a fiery pain in his shoulder and ribs when he tried to move. Thuyet pushed him down.

"Remain still! An ambulance is coming," she said. "We think your shoulder is broken."

Linh's eyes were sparkling. "Kien, you were so brave!"

More foolish than brave, Kien thought. To think that he had tried to save Orrin, knowing what the big man had done! It was such an unbelievable thought that Kien closed his eyes again. As he did so, he felt a sudden patter of water on his face.

"It has begun to rain," Thuyet announced in a satisfied voice. "Now the fire will go out. The fire department will have the help of Heaven."

The ambulance came a few minutes later. Kien was loaded on board, next to a groaning Orrin. Kien moaned, too, as he was lifted into the ambulance. "How are you doing, buddy?" the ambulance attendant asked.

Linh answered for him. "Kien is badly hurt. He was the one who went into the fire to save Orrin."

"What! This kid?" The ambulance attendant was impressed. "After all the things Paul said about you people?"

The ambulance took off in a scream of sound. In spite of his hurts, Kien was delighted as they tore through Travor at a dizzying pace, the sirens wailing. And as they rattled along, Kien had an idea. The attendant had been impressed by his trying to save Orrin. Linh had said he was brave. Perhaps, if he was careful and clever, something could be made from this situation. Perhaps he could bring peace to Travor after all . . . on his own terms!

Kien was so excited about this idea that he hardly felt pain when the ambulance attendant unloaded him at Travor Hospital. The man misunderstood Kien's silence. "Little buddy, are you okay?" he asked worriedly. To the orderlies who took charge of Kien, he explained, "This kid tried to save Paul Orrin from a burning boat. Imagine, this little kid!"

Now, Kien was certain that his idea would work! He closed his eyes, wrenched his face into a grimace of pain, and gave a heartrending groan. "Hurt," he whispered. "I hurt . . ."

"We'll take care of you right away," the orderly promised. Carefully, almost reverently, he transferred

Kien to a stretcher. "Little guy, you are a gutsy one, I'll tell you that!"

Shortly afterward, Kien was examined by a young doctor. "Hurts, does it?" he asked. "It should. You have a fractured collarbone and bruised ribs. Your hair and eyelashes are singed off and you've got burns on your hands and arms. But that's nothing to what could have happened to you. What made you go after Paul Orrin, of all people? I heard that he was dead set on scaring the Vietnamese out of Travor."

Kien slit open his eyes and whispered in a die-away voice, "We are all . . . men. My people . . . couldn't watch Orrin die. People should . . . live and work to-gether."

The young doctor looked very impressed. Now, Kien thought, I hope he tells other people what I have said. He groaned again, most convincingly.

The doctor was saying, "That's what I've always said. Live and let live. I never agreed with Orrin. After all, America was made by immigrants."

Kien felt so pleased he could have jumped off the ex-amination table and danced around. Instead, he gave a few more sorrowful moans. The young nurse who was assisting the doctor had tears in her eyes.

"It must hurt terribly," she whispered. "Oh, you poor, brave boy!"

Kien was then wheeled up to the third floor of the hospital to the pediatrics ward. Here, news of his ex-ploits had already reached the nurses at their third-floor station. They made a big fuss over Kien and told the other children in the ward that he was a hero.

"If it hadn't been for Kien, Mr. Paul Orrin might have been killed," one of the nurses said. "We heard it on the radio news, just now."

The children were impressed. So were the nurses. Let *them* tell others, Kien thought. He moaned aloud, think-ing, You have your tricks, Mr. Paul Orrin, I have mine. Let's see who wins in the end!

The nurse patted and pampered Kien for some time,

then gave him something that would relax him. He was grateful for this, because his shoulder and chest truly did hurt. After a while, he felt a warmth and stillness creep through his whole body, and his eyelids became so heavy that he closed them. But he could not have closed them for long. Was he not looking at Teacher Van Chi, who was standing right there in the hospital beside his bed?

"My grandson," the old man was saying, "you see now that I was right. We must repay evil with good, for good is always stronger. Evil can almost always be turned to good."

"Grandfather, I've missed you . . ." and then Kien stopped, remembering that he had thrown away the precious bag of sand. But the old teacher seemed to understand all about that.

"I know you have tried to leave your family, Kien, but you never really have succeeded," he said gently. "It is time for you to go home."

"But I have no home!" Kien cried. Suddenly, the scene shifted. He was standing by the pier, looking out to sea. A large, silver-finned fish came swimming through the waves toward him.

"Hello, Kien," the big fish called. "I'm a salmon and I'm on my way home."

"I don't know where my home is," Kien sighed.

"Nonsense! You've known all along!" The silver-finned fish laughed and disappeared back into the water.

"Wait!" Kien called. "Don't go!"

"You don't have to yell. I'm not going anywhere," a familiar voice said. "I'm right here, Kien." Kien blinked open his eyes and saw sunlight glinting on Bill Ransom's red beard. "I stopped by to see if you'd woken up yet." Bill smiled. "That stuff they gave you must have been pretty powerful. You've been asleep the whole night and for part of today, too."

Kien blinked again. Sunlight slanted through the hospital windows. He could hear children's voices all around, laughing and talking with visitors. He started to sit up, then groaned in very real pain.

"Easy," Bill cautioned. "You won't be able to run around for quite a while." He dropped a newspaper onto Kien's bed. "Look at that. While you've been lying here, you've become a hero!"

Kien looked at the local newspaper, the *Travor Tribune*. "Picture of me!" he exclaimed.

"Sure it is. Know what the article under the photo says?"

"No, please read!" Kien begged. Bill cleared his throat.

"A young Vietnamese boy saved Paul Orrin from death when the latter's boat caught fire Thursday afternoon," he read. "Both Orrin and young Kien, age 15, were taken to Travor Hospital to be treated for smoke inhalation and other injuries. Asked why he risked his life to help Orrin, Kien said, 'All people should work and live together.'"

Kien grinned all over his face. This was even better than he had expected.

"You look pleased," Bill smiled. "The nurses and doctor tell me you're in terrible pain. Are you feeling better?"

Kien considered, then decided to tell Bill his plan. "Bill, it hurt, but not bad like I pretend," he confessed. As Bill's eyebrows rose in surprise, he added, "I have plan. Big plan. I think maybe, if it work, everyone happy and Bác Huy get back boats."

Bill tugged his beard thoughtfully. "That's a tall order, Kien." Then he leaned forward. "What do you have in mind?"

"I need talk Orrin alone. I need tell him some things." Kien decided he needn't tell Bill about Orrin's setting fire to his own boat. "Then, I need help. Need to get Bác Huy and Orrin together. Talk together. That is hard."

"I think so, too." Bill looked thoughtful. "How's this? Bác Huy and Phat are busy packing today. I'll bring them to the hospital to see you an hour from now. Orrin

was up and around this morning. Ask a nurse to fetch
him to see you in about fifty minutes."

Kien nodded, eyes glinting. "Sure. Look bad if he not
come see me," he agreed. "Don't forget, Bill! Bring Bác
Huy and Phat in hour!"

The minutes crept by. Kien rehearsed what he was
going to say. The words came slowly to his mind, and he
turned each word over carefully. Finally, Kien asked a
nurse to fetch Orrin to him.

"I need . . . see him," Kien groaned in a die-away
voice, and the nurse hurried away.

When Paul Orrin came to the room, Kien didn't recog-
nize him at first. Orrin's eyebrows and eyelashes had
been burned away, and a bandage covered his bruised
head. His eyes, however, were as Kien remembered—
gray, intolerant, and just now, uneasy.

He doesn't like that I helped save his life, Kien
thought. Aloud, he said, "How you feel, Mr. Orrin?"

Orrin cleared his throat uncomfortably. "I hear that
you helped me out yesterday," he rumbled. "I always
pay my debts, sonny. If you want something—"

"I want," Kien interrupted. "I want you tear up paper
that say you buy boats from Vietnamese."

Orrin stared. After a while, he began to laugh. "You're
joking!"

"Is not joke. Mr. Orrin, think about it. If you try run
Vietnamese out of Travor right now, you look bad. I
hero!"

Orrin's eyes narrowed. "So. Your hurt hero act was a
big lie, wasn't it?" Kien smiled. "It won't work, sonny. I
have no intention of giving up those boats."

"Mr. Orrin, you listen. Suppose I speak about fire on
your boat, one you blame Phat for burning. How many
will believe me?" Kien demanded.

"Not many!" Orrin shot back. "Most of the people
around here owe me money or work for me. They respect me."

"Not respect if they know what you do. They may

think, If he cheat Vietnamese, he cheat us too, some-day!"

For a second, a look of fear filled Orrin's deep-set eyes. "You have no proof!" he snapped. "Why would I set fire to my own boat?"

"You want Vietnamese look bad, get rid of them from town," Kien said. "You afraid Vietnamese stay, you no make money on fish. Is foolish. Plenty fish. You sit down, talk with Vietnamese, they talk with you. Both listen."

Orrin turned away. "You're wasting your time, sonny," he said.

"Then, Mr. Orrin, I tell Phat and Bác Huy what I know. I tell Bill Ransom. Go to police."

"No one would believe you!"

"You sure, Mr. Orrin?" Kien challenged. "Vietnamese don't have much to lose. You have plenty. And me—I am hero, remember?"

Orrin glared at Kien for a moment. Then, he gave a short bark of laughter. "Sonny, it appears that I underestimated you. Suppose, for a moment, that I *do* give back Huy Dao and the others their boats. Then what?"

Kien cried eagerly, "You work with each other! Can do! Can make Travor good place for everyone!"

Orrin frowned. Then he shook his head. "Dao would never work with me. He hates my guts."

There was a soft knock on the door. Phat, followed by Bác Huy and Bill, walked into the room. When the Vietnamese saw Orrin, they turned away.

"We will return later," Phat snapped.

This was going to be the hardest part of all, Kien realized. "No. Please come in," he begged.

Bill cleared his throat. "Phat, I have to confess that Kien asked me to bring you and your uncle here to speak with Paul. He asks that you listen to what he has to say."

Phat translated, and Kien held his breath. Then Bác Huy nodded. "Very well, I will listen. I should have gone after Orrin yesterday, instead of this boy. Kien was hurt because of this. I owe him enough to listen, but that is all I will do."

"Travor is a good place to live," Kien began. His voice quavered, and his heart was beating so hard that it seemed as if his chest was jumping. "Orrin has agreed to . . . to return the paper that says you sold him the boats. I think he will be willing to work with you and the other Vietnamese fishermen."

Bác Huy's fierce eyes looked ready to shoot thunderbolts. "I will never work with this one!" he shouted.

Orrin smiled sourly. "No need for you to translate," he said. "There's no way that Huy Dao and I can work together."

Bill shook his head. "That isn't going to get you anywhere, Paul. You people wouldn't cooperate before, and look what happened." He turned to Phat. "Phat, Orrin was wrong, but that doesn't mean you have to be wrong, too. If you want the happiness of your people, you must listen."

Kien added in Vietnamese, "Linh likes Travor, Bác Huy. Aunt Thuyet calls it home . . ." His voice seemed small and weak in the silence. Bác Huy's face paled, then reddened.

"How do we know Orrin will keep his promises?" he asked at last. "He may give back our boats and then . . . and then try some underhanded way of getting rid of us again!"

Bill shook his head when his remark was translated. "Paul will keep his promise. I talked to a lot of people today, and they are nearly all in favor of the Vietnamese staying." He turned to Orrin. "Paul, the people of Travor went along with you because they either worked for you, or owed you money, or respected you. Now, they sympathize with the Vietnamese. If you try and push the Vietnamese around anymore, the town will turn on you."

While Phat was translating this, Orrin spoke in his deep voice. "I know when I'm up against a wall, Bill Ransom," he boomed. "I'm also a businessman." He turned to Bác Huy and held out his hand. "If you'll work with me, Huy Dao, I'll try and meet you halfway," he said.

Bác Huy just stared at Orrin's big hand. Please, Kien thought, please.

Then, very slowly, the little Vietnamese took Orrin's hand in his. "Travor my home," he said in English. "Okay. We try work together!"

16

"I won't go to school," Kien said defiantly. "He can't make me, Bill."

It was three weeks later, and Kien was sitting in Bill Ransom's small but comfortable living room. Outside, the summer sun beat down on lazy Travor streets, and out at sea fishing craft chugged peacefully. Bill smiled at Kien's rebellious face.

"Why not try it?"

"I not want! I hate school. I hate it back in—" Kien stopped. He had almost said, "Back in Bradley."

"Well, it might be different here," Bill pointed out. "People think the world of you here in Travor, Kien."

Kien should have been pleased by this, but the pleasure did not lighten the heaviness he felt. Surely he should take pride in what he had helped to do, Kien thought.

The town's feelings about the Vietnamese had changed. The townspeople had gone to the Vietnamese community with offers of food, clothing, help. Teenagers who had jeered and attacked Kien and the other children now came forward to help sweep up glass, put up new windows, paint, rebuild. As they grew to know one another, they were beginning to be friends.

Orrin's fishermen now sat down to talk with the Viet-

namese. Together, the two groups agreed to set a price
limit, so that no one could undercut the other. They
agreed on a limit to the number of fish any one fisherman could sell. Though they often argued heatedly, they
hammered out their differences with words.

I had something to do with that, Kien thought, and up
till now I have been treated like a man. Why, then, does
Bác Huy talk about sending me to school like a child?

Last night, Bác Huy had approached him. "It's time to
think about your future, Kien," he had said. "Now that
peace has come back to our town, it is time to consider
important things like knowledge, and education."

Kien did not like the way the little leader looked at
him. "I don't think I am quite well enough to go to
school," he had hedged.

"Nonsense!" Thuyet had snorted at once. "You must
go to Linh's school. There are good teachers there and
they will teach you young ones how to have better lives
than us old people." She had looked proud and determined. "Don't argue," she had scolded Kien.

Then Bác Huy had added the clincher. "After all, you
must set an example for the young Vietnamese," he had
said smugly. "They look up to you. Now that you are a
part of this family."

I do not have a family! Kien had wanted to cry. I am
free! And, he had thought, Now it is definitely time to
leave Travor and move on!

Yet here he was sitting in Bill Ransom's living room. It
was not easy to move on, after all. "What's the trouble,
Kien?" Bill asked, and then added with a smile, "Getting
itchy feet again?"

"Itchy?"

Bill explained, and Kien nodded slowly. "Maybe so,
Bill. But where I go? America a big place." He sighed.

Bill smiled. "Maybe you want to settle down in Travor
for a while. Bác Huy and Thuyet think of you as part of
their family, and Linh and Phat are very fond of you."

Kien did not answer. He didn't want to stay in Travor.

It was a fine place, now, and yet he did not want to live here. Nor did he want to leave. It was very upsetting.

"Do you know what's wrong with you?" Bill was asking. "You're homesick!"

"I not having home."

"Think about it, Kien," Bill advised.

Kien walked away from Bill's house feeling even more unhappy and unsettled. *Think about it.* Sometimes, Bill sounded just like Steve Olson.

"No," Kien told himself out loud. He didn't want to think of the Olsons. He didn't want to think of anything. His healed collarbone itched, and he felt fuzzy-headed and empty inside, as if some part of him was missing.

Kien walked into the sunlit street. High over his head in the blue Travor sky flew a small red kite. As Kien watched, the kite bobbed and then soared even higher. "Just like the dragon kite I bought Loc in Hong Kong," Kien murmured. "He really did love that kite . . ."

And then, suddenly, he could see Loc running, playing with Tad. Steve Olson, too . . . Kien could feel the pressure of Steve's hand on his shoulder. He started to walk quickly, but not quickly enough to escape remembering the way Diane worried about him, or the way she used to bake special brownies just for him. And Mai . . .

"Mai," Kien whispered and felt the emptiness inside him grow so that he could hardly bear it.

In his dream, Grandfather Van Chi had said that Kien had never left his family. It was true. He had thought of these beloved people all during the time he was in Travor. He did not need the bag of Vietnamese sand to remind him of his bond with them.

Mai cried when I phoned her, he thought. I should go back. But then he remembered why he had left Bradley in the first place. Sim Evans did not frighten him anymore. After all, he had handled Paul Orrin and one foolish red-haired bully would be very little trouble. But what of Mai and the others?

If my being there is going to hurt them, if they're better off without me, I can always leave again, Kien said to himself. I don't need . . . He had started to say, I don't need anyone, but the words stuck in his throat. I don't need to stay long if I don't want to, he thought.

That night, he told Bác Huy and his family about his decision. Linh cried. "Why do you have to leave?" she sobbed. Phat and Bác Huy, however, understood.

"It is something Kien must do before he can be happy," Phat told Linh and Thuyet.

"Suppose they do not want you back?" Thuyet demanded. She was ready to cry herself, and for this reason she was angry with everyone. "Kien, if you don't like things back there, you must come back here! I insist!"

Kien wanted to slip away without saying anything to the Vietnamese community, but this was impossible. Thuyet had a party, to which Bill Ransom was invited, and they ate and sang songs and even shed a few tears. In many ways, it made Kien feel sad to be leaving Travor.

The next day, Kien said his good-bys and walked to the bus depot with Bác Huy's family and Bill Ransom. "We're sorry to see you go," Bill said, "and we'll always be glad to see you come back this way. Happy landings, Kien."

What were happy landings? Kien did not know. He waved to all his friends, clutched the bus ticket for which Bác Huy had insisted on paying, and climbed onto the bus. He did not know whether he was happy or sad, and his stomach flip-flopped like a salmon on its voyage back to its birthplace.

The bus rolled on. Kien slept . . . stopped to eat . . . slept again. When the big bus finally slid into Bradley, it was night.

Kien shouldered his bag and began to walk toward the Olson home. It was a fine night, and the sky was washed with stars. As Kien tramped the familiar roads that would lead him to the Olson house, he felt his heart begin to thump against his ribs.

It is nothing to get excited about, he told himself sternly. I am here just to see how everyone is. That's all.

Then the Olson house stood before him, silent and asleep. He looked at the dark building, and his courage failed. "Maybe it would be better if I never went in," Kien whispered.

Yet he walked up the front steps and to the door. It was locked, but Kien had never worried about locked doors. He pulled a flat playing card from his pocket and slid it up the crack of the door, springing the lock.

He went inside. The familiar hallway greeted him. He had not expected to feel like this. He had not expected that the place would affect him physically. He saw the flowers in the living room, Loc's and Tad's toys, a book of Mai's open on the coffee table.

I am only here to see how they are, Kien told himself. If they don't need me, I'll go on. I'll have plenty of adventures.

Yet he wanted to stay. He hadn't known how badly, and it scared him. He almost turned to the door to leave, but suddenly a familiar smell drew him down the hallway and into the kitchen.

The kitchen was lighted by a night-light plugged into the wall. The night-light shed its glow on the kitchen table. There, standing at his place on the table was his own dish. And on that dish was a mound of freshly baked chocolate-chip brownies.

Kien set his bag down. His hands were shaking and his eyes blurred with tears. For a moment, till he could control his feelings, he remained very still, very quiet, letting the welcoming smell of the brownies enfold him. Then he reached out and picked up a brownie and put it into his mouth.

It tasted of home.

VIETNAMESE WORDS

Bác	Uncle—a term of respect for an older man
Cam vao	Keep out!
Lua chay	Stop!
Nung lai	Teacher
Thay	Enough!
Thoi dii	Fire!
Tieng chao buoi sang	Good morning
Tuy ong	As you like

ABOUT THE AUTHOR

MAUREEN CRANE WARTSKI was born in Ashiya, Japan, and lived there until she was seventeen. She attended the University of Redlands in California and Sophia University in Tokyo.

A writer since she sold her first story at age fourteen, she often writes about the many countries she has visited, especially the countries of Southeast Asia. She has also taught English and history overseas, and in Sharon, Massachusetts, where she lives with her husband, Mike, and their sons Bert and Mark.

Her first novel, MY BROTHER IS SPECIAL, is also available in Signet paperback, as is her prize-winning second novel, A BOAT TO NOWHERE.

There's an epidemic with 27 million victims. And no visible symptoms.

It's an epidemic of people who can't read.

Believe it or not, 27 million Americans are functionally illiterate, about one adult in five.

The solution to this problem is you... when you join the fight against illiteracy. So call the Coalition for Literacy at toll-free **1-800-228-8813** and volunteer.

Volunteer Against Illiteracy. The only degree you need is a degree of caring.